Prep Cool

Read all the Cinderella Cleaners books!

MAYA GOLD

SCHOLASTIC INC.

New York   Toronto   London   Auckland
Sydney   Mexico City   New Delhi   Hong Kong

ISBN: 978-0-545-12960-2

12 11 10 9 8 7 6 5 4 3 2   10 11 12 13 14 15/0

Printed in the U.S.A.
First edition, April 2010

Book design by Yaffa Jaskoll

For M. S. S.
I love you old-school

Acknowledgments

Grateful thanks to my wonderful editor, Aimee Friedman, and to Becky Shapiro, for their insight and encouragement, and to my daughter Sophia and her friends at Rondout Valley Middle School and High School for correcting my paper on fashion, slang, music, texting, and everything under the teenage sun. I'm listening!

Prep Cool

Chapter One

Nothing feels better than walking outside after school. You're surrounded by friends, and everyone's talking at once, and you're *moving*, not sitting in rows while some teacher drones on. You step through the door, and the sun hits your face, and the yellow school buses are lined up, and the October leaves are sixteen shades of gorgeous. What can be bad?

Two words: French test.

Make it three: French test *tomorrow*.

The textbook sits in my backpack like a tombstone. My best friend, Jessica Munson, is walking ahead of me, noisily shuffling her sneakers through leaves, not a care in the world. This is because Jess, like the rest of my friends and anyone sane, takes Spanish instead of La Torture Chamber

1

of Madame Lefkowitz. As soon as my teacher gave us a list of subjects the test's going to cover, my stomach started to feel heavy. Why do verbs come in *irregular* anyway? It makes them sound like they're jeans with a defect.

Jess jumps off the curb and into a pile of dry leaves at the edge of the parking lot. The sun glints off her springy red hair. "Come on, Diana!" she yells, and I can't resist jumping in after her. Jess always manages to lighten things up and make me feel better. We're kicking big piles of leaves at each other when Kayleigh Carell, the reigning queen of the eighth grade, turns to her permanent sidekick, Savannah, and says, "Ever notice how *some* people still act like toddlers?"

Savannah covers a fake giggle with her hand. "Burn!"

Better than acting like mean-girl snobs, I want to yell back, but getting in Kayleigh's face is never a good thing to do. Especially since she's going out with Ethan Horowitz, a boy Jess and I have been friends with forever. Most of the time, Kayleigh pretends to be nice to us for Ethan's sake, and because we're all in the drama club. But it's a little like watching a snake try to smile.

Kayleigh runs her eyes over my vintage corduroy jacket and stares at my Converse high-tops, which are laced up in two different colors, as always. Today they're yellow and orange: my fall foliage look. Kayleigh lifts her nose into the air and practically sniffs as she passes. She and Savannah are both wearing white quilted jackets from Hollister and light-wash jeans tucked into Ugg boots. The only way you can tell which one is which from the back is that Kayleigh's ponytail is blonder.

"Please tell me she's not on our bus," Jess says under her breath.

"She's not," I reply. "Got your bus pass?"

Jess and I both live close enough to walk home from school, but back in September, my stepmother decided I had to help out after school at my father's dry cleaners. The timing could not have been worse: I wasn't allowed to be in the fall play, which was beyond disappointing. But my job turned out to have a real silver lining: Because of it, I got to sneak into the opening night of the world's most amazing Broadway musical, *Angel*, starring my number one celebrity crush, Adam Kessler. And I even got to *meet* Adam after the show and dance with him under the stars! None of that would have happened at all if I wasn't working at Cinderella Cleaners, so I'm cool with it now.

Today, Jess is taking the bus to work with me for the first time. She's been dying to visit, but up till this week she's been tied up with rehearsals and chores for her mom. Now she's got a free afternoon to hang out, and wouldn't you know it, I'm drowning in French verbs to study. I wonder how you say "This totally stinks" *en francais*.

We're passing the flagpole. If you sat on the top and looked down at all the kids streaming out of Weehawken Middle School, crisscrossing the parking lot onto their various buses, it would probably look like a roller derby. It's amazing we don't all crash into each other. As Jess and I thread through the pack toward bus 26A, someone jogs over to us. It's Will Carson, a new boy who's in my English class. He also works on the stage crew in drama club.

"Guess what," he says, bouncing up onto the toes of his sneakers.

"I don't know, what?" Jess's voice is sarcastic but friendly; she and Will are buddies.

Will's so excited, he circles in front of us and starts walking backward. He's wearing a Death Cab for Cutie T-shirt and his dark hair tumbles over his forehead. He's grinning from ear to ear, and I notice, not for the first time, that he might be a little bit cute. Not Adam Kessler or Robert Pattinson cute, but not bad for an eighth-grade boy.

"I got a gig! A real one, for money!"

"No way!" Jess stops walking so suddenly that I slam into her back. I flush with embarrassment.

"Really?" I ask Will, though, duh, he just said so.

Will nods happily. "With my brother's band. They're playing a dance at the Foreman Academy Saturday night, and yesterday their bass player broke two of his fingers at football practice. So my brother just asked me to cover."

"Like in *42nd Street*!" I blurt. Oh, God, did I really say that out loud?

Will looks confused, but before I can tell him that it's a musical where the star breaks her leg and the understudy gets to go on in her place, Jess says, "The Foreman Academy?" with so much awe in her voice you'd think Will just told her he's playing on *MTV*

Live. "You mean Preppy Palace? I hope they're paying you tons!"

"You know what, I never asked." Will shrugs. "I was so stoked the rest of the band thinks I'm good enough, but yeah, right, I guess." This sounds more like the Will Carson I know from English class, so shy that his thoughts dangle off in mid-sentence. The first few weeks of school, I thought he was a mute.

"What's the Foreman Academy?" I ask Jess.

"Oh, come on, you must have passed it a million times," Jess says. "It's a fancy boarding school in, like, this *castle* high up on the Palisades," Jess says. "It's behind a big fence? Near the overlook point?"

I'm still not getting a picture. She sighs. "You're probably daydreaming about some show every time you drive by it. And you can't see the actual school from the road. It's hidden away from us peasants. I heard that going there costs more than most colleges."

"Whatever," says Will. "The band's really cool. They're all juniors and seniors. The lead singer sounds like Pink."

"We *have* to come see you." Jess folds her arms, setting her jaw in an I-won't-take-no-for-an-answer position.

Will hesitates. "I think the dance is for Foreman Academy students only."

"Okay, we'll come early and carry equipment," says Jess, and I wish I could step on her foot. How obvious is it that Will doesn't want to bring two eighth-grade girls to his first paying gig with a cool high school band? He shifts his backpack from one shoulder to the other but doesn't say anything.

"Tell me you don't get to bring a few guests. Bands *always* get to bring guests," says Jess. "We'll be your fan club."

Will looks so uncomfortable that the warning blasts from the school buses' air horns feel like an answered prayer. I grab Jess's hand, pulling her toward our bus as I yell to Will over my shoulder, "Later, okay?"

Jess and I argue about the Foreman dance all the way down to the waterfront, where there's a beautiful view of the Statue of Liberty and New York Harbor. There are a couple of really steep hills, and every time the bus driver rolls down one, the fifth-grade boys make roller coaster sounds of "WwwhOOOa!" and throw spitballs across the aisle. It's completely annoying.

"But Will doesn't *want* us to go. It was totally obvious."

"No way," says Jess. "He's just being a boy."

"What does *that* mean?"

"That he's secretly happy I asked, but he can't let us know that because it's not cool, so he's acting like he's saying no, but he really means yes."

"That's ridiculous!"

"I have a brother," Jess says darkly. "I know how their twisted minds work."

Our back-and-forth could easily go on forever, but we've reached our stop. Up ahead I can see the neon crown on the roof of Cinderella Cleaners, right next door to the shiny chrome and turquoise trim of Sam's Diner. We step onto the curb and start walking toward the cleaners.

"So I'm finally getting to meet all these supercool people you talk about all the time," says Jess.

"Not *all* the time."

"Almost. More than you talk about drama club."

"I can't *go* to drama club, hello. Anyway, you're not doing anything now except planning the holiday show. Which I won't be in either, so don't rub it in."

"Sorry," says Jess, looking up at the crown. "Wow. I haven't been here since your grandfather owned it. Does it still have those gumball machines in the lobby?"

"Gumballs and Skittles."

"Do you get them free?"

I laugh. "What do you think?"

"When I get a job," says Jess, "I will *insist* on free candy."

"You do that. Tell your boss to throw in a free car while you're at it."

"With a chauffeur," Jess says. "Like the guy who drove you to see *Angel*. Mom and I had to go on the PATH train."

Thanks to my little escapade at *Angel*, Adam Kessler sent two front-row tickets to raffle off at the fall play, and Jess won. She went to a matinee with her mother last weekend, and ever since then, she's been starstruck. "Don't you wish you could see Broadway shows every night and go home in a stretch limo?"

As usual, Jess makes me laugh. "As if!" I say.

"Did I tell you the restaurant Mom and I ate in —"

"You've told me five times."

"The food was *so* good." Jess sighs.

Jess's mom is divorced and works hard as a nurse, but when Jess won the tickets, Mrs. Munson took her to lunch at a four-star French restaurant near the theatre. They split one entree and one salad, and splurged on dessert. "It was so worth it," Jess tells me, again. "Forget your Madame Lefkowitz troubles. Any country that came up with crème brûlée is fine by me. Hey, where are you going?"

I've passed by the cleaners' front door and am heading around to the back of the building. "Employee entrance," I grin. "We're going *backstage.*"

"Cool!" says Jess.

The back door to Cinderella Cleaners is, in fact, a bit like a stage door, leading onto a hallway with doors to the dressing rooms and the coffee and soda machines. There's even a sort of costume rack, full of the pastel green smocks the employees have to wear. I swipe my card through the time clock and pick up my smock.

"Should I wear one, too?" Jess asks.

I hesitate. "Better not. MacInerny will bark at you." Miss MacInerny is my supervisor. She's a thin, birdlike woman whose mouth is pulled down in a permanent frown. Of all inappropriate things, her first name is Joy. My friends at the customer counter and I call her Joyless, or Mac Attack.

Jess and I head into the women's locker room and bump right into one of those friends, Elise Andrews. She's a junior at Hoboken High School. She's already wearing her name tag and smock and pulling her long blond hair into a ponytail. She smiles at Jess. "Are you training?"

Jess looks confused. "Um, no, I'm just —"

"Jess is my best friend," I say quickly. "She's just hanging out."

"Oh, sorry," Elise says. "I thought you'd been hired to take over my job during basketball season. Practice starts in two weeks. I'm Elise."

"And I'm Cat," says the petite, dark-haired girl who's just entered the dressing room. "We're the after-school Three Musketeers. You've gotta be Jess with that hair."

Jess gives me the eye, but looks secretly pleased. "You've been *talking* about me?"

"Yeah, yeah, it's all good," says Cat, peeling her peacoat off and hanging it inside a locker. "Who's got first shift at the customer counter?"

"You do, Catalina," Elise says, and Cat rolls her eyes.

"Great. I am *so* up for working with Joyless today." She watches me pin my name tag on my smock. "Did you tell her you're bringing a guest?"

"I asked my father to tell her."

"Oh, she's gonna have a cow. Good times!" Cat grins, snaps up her green smock, turns, and pushes into the work-room. As soon as the door opens, Jess claps her hands to her ears, and I remember how loud the machine noise seemed to me just a few weeks ago. Elise told me back then I'd get used to it, and I guess I did.

Elise takes something plaid out of a shopping bag,

followed by something navy blue. "What's that?" I ask, ever curious.

"My cousin's school uniform. She spilled paint on it, and asked me to drop it off for stain removal. See you in a few!" Elise gives Jess a warm smile and carries the bunched-up uniform into the workroom.

Jess doesn't cover her ears this time, but her eyebrows arch even higher. "And I thought the woodshop for stage crew was noisy!"

"Oh, we're heavy metal over here," I say, closing my locker. "You ready?"

"One second." Jess whips out her new bright red cell phone and snaps a quick photo of me in my pastel green smock with the name tag pinned under the dorky gold crown.

"You show that to anyone and you're *dead*!"

"Who would I show it to? Will?" Jess laughs. "Kayleigh Carell?"

"I'll kill you nine times, I'm not kidding."

"Relax. It's for my eyes only," says Jess. "I promise not to post it on Facebook for all to admire." I grab at the phone and she holds it above her head, laughing and snapping a second shot of me lunging toward it.

"Not fair!" I know she's just kidding, but I'm still alarmed. I would be *so* embarrassed if anyone saw that.

"Hey, Diana. Rewind," Jess says soothingly. "Look, I'm going to delete it, okay? Watch me press DELETE." She does, twice, and my body relaxes.

"*Thank* you," I say.

"What are friends for?" Jess smirks. She carefully places her phone in the outside zipper pocket of her hobo bag and looks at me. "Will this be safe in your locker?"

"Of course."

"Did I tell you I love my new phone?"

"Only about six million times," I say, twisting the lock shut. "You ready?"

"You bet!"

I push the door open. The workroom is busy as ever. Picture the world's biggest closet, with a flock of people in pale green smocks hanging dresses on hangers and steam-pressing trousers and sorting huge mounds of clothes into laundry machines. There's a radio pumping out music on top of the waves of machine noise, and high

14

overhead is a moving conveyor belt carrying garments in clear plastic bags.

"Whoa!" says Jess, her head swiveling back and forth. "This is *so cool*! It's like Santa's workshop with clothes!"

I would have to agree. If you're into fashion and costumes like I am, the back of a cleaners *is* kind of magical.

I show Jess the No Pickup rack, where cleaned clothes get stored if they haven't been claimed within thirty days. If they stay on the rack thirty *more* days, they're given to charity — or to employees.

"It's like a free thrift store!" says Jess. "One-stop shopping for Halloween costumes."

Halloween is still three weeks away, but we're already planning our outfits. I want to be zombie lunch ladies, but Jess favors punk-rocker fairies. She fingers a black leather jacket. "This would be *perfect*."

"Don't even think about that," says a cheerful voice right behind us. "Six more days and that jacket is *mine*." It's Chris, the maintenance guy. His name is Chris Dowling, but he likes to say he's Chris Rock but less rich. I introduce Jess, and he says, "You got great taste. But I got there first, you hear?"

Jess laughs; I knew she'd like everyone here.

Well, almost everyone.

I want to show Jess my other favorite place, the climate-controlled vault where we store things like fur coats and luxury goods. But I have the feeling she's going to go crazy in there, and I know if we dawdle too long, MacInerny will be even angrier at me for bringing a friend.

"Follow me," I shout over the noise, and we head down the aisle between workstations. I introduce Jess to the elderly man at the steam presser, Mr. Chen, but his wife, Rose, is out sick today. We thread our way past the sorting table and bagging machine, then push open the double doors into the customer section. It's like leaving a noisy restaurant kitchen and coming out into the dining room. This part of the building is light-filled and airy, with big plate-glass windows. Cat's logging a new order into the computer, and Miss MacInerny is handing a customer change from the cash register. As soon as she sees me with Jess, her perma-frown irons into an angry straight line.

"Who's this? What are you doing back here?" she snaps.

Cat turns her head toward us, mouthing "I told you so."

I can feel my ears burning. "My father said —"

"Employees-only behind the counter. You know the rules." It's amazing how someone so small can command such authority. She's like one of those terriers that bark at dogs twice their size.

I flip up the hinged section of counter, and Jess follows me through. From the customer side, I tell Joyless, "This is Jessica Munson. My father told you she'd be coming today."

MacInerny shoots me a look that would petrify snakes, and I realize I've made a bad thing worse. She's never approved of me working here in the first place, and mentioning my father is not going to help. Too late, though: The door to Dad's office is open, and out he comes.

"I may not have remembered to tell you," he says, "but yes, I did give Diana permission to bring her best friend to visit this afternoon. Welcome, Jess!"

"Thanks, Mr. Donato," says Jess, sounding uncharacteristically meek.

But MacInerny's not finished. She turns to Jess, pasting on a fake smile for Dad's sake. "There are safety issues involved. I'm sure you can appreciate that."

Jess nods. "My mom works in a hospital lab. I'll be supersafe."

"'Course she will." Dad beams. "Jess isn't going to *work* with Diana, she's just going to take a quick tour and then sit up front and do homework. Frankly, I don't see the problem."

Before MacInerny can come up with an answer to that, I grab Jess by the hand and say, "Come and see Tailoring."

The three tailors have their own glassed-in area, off to one side of the customer counter. It's full of bright swatches of cloth, rows of thread, and the comforting clatter of sewing machines. The two seamstresses, Sadie and Loretta, have both worked here forever. My grandfather brought me to meet them when I was a baby, and they love to tell me how they stitched my crib quilt.

The head tailor, Nelson Martinez, is young enough to be their grandson, but nobody has any doubts he's the boss. He's an amazing designer — he's saving up money for graduate school, but his biggest dream is to win *Project*

Runway. He's actually gone to try out for it twice. Nelson made drop-dead gorgeous dresses for me and Cat when we went to the *Angel* premiere. Jess knows the whole story, but I've made her swear up and down she won't breathe a word to anyone.

Today, Nelson is bent over the cutting table, working his shears around pattern pieces with the confidence of a chef. He's wearing a pin-striped vest over a T-shirt and black jeans, topped off with a hip-hop fedora. He straightens up when he sees Jess.

"Amy Adams!"

"Excuse me?" says Jess.

Nelson takes a step back, looking her up and down. "Five foot three?" he says, and Jess nods. "Perfect."

"This is Jess, by the way," I say, then tell my BFF, "Nelson doesn't believe in hellos."

"*Hola*," says Nelson impatiently. "Would you model a gown for me?"

Jess's eyes get big. "Sure!"

Nelson goes over to one of the dressmaker's forms, from which he unpins a poufy white gown with a full skirt. "A customer asked me to copy a dress from *Enchanted*. The sleeves look like deflated volleyballs, but that's what she wants. Dressing room is right there." He pushes the gown into Jess's arms, sending her into the curtained booth next to the three-way mirror.

"Who would order a gown from *Enchanted*?" I ask.

Nelson shrugs. "It's for some Halloween charity ball at Newark Performing Arts Center."

I'm stunned. "A hand-tailored dress for a Halloween costume?"

"Rich people are different, *amiga*. Hey, how's it going in there?" he calls into the dressing room.

"Good," Jess's voice comes out muffled. "Except there's no zipper."

"Work in progress. I'll pin you."

"Okay," says Jess. She pulls back the curtain and steps out uncertainly. Sadie clasps her hands over her heart.

"You look like a movie star," she says, and Loretta echoes, "Bee-yootiful!"

"Those sleeves should be shot," Nelson says. "I'm just following orders. Step up on that stool and I'll pin up the hem."

As I watch him at work, I can't help remembering the way I felt wearing the black-and-white satin dress Nelson made me for *Angel,* and that incredible dance I shared with Adam Kessler. *Why can't life be like that all the time?* I think as I picture us whirling together in a moonlit garden. It's all I can do not to sigh.

"That was awesome!" Jess cries as she follows me back to the workroom. I'm pushing a rolling bin full of tagged clothes, having promised Miss MacInerny that Jess won't touch anything in the back room. Since I'm technically too young to run the cash register or work with the heavy machines, most of my job is delivering clothes from one room to another and hanging things up. It's a little like being a busboy before you're a waiter.

"Can you believe someone's buying that gown for a charity ball?" says Jess.

"*I* want to go to a ball," I say dreamily, thinking of Adam.

"Maybe Nelson will make you a dress for the Foreman Academy dance."

I stop pushing the cart. "We aren't invited, okay? Will does not want us to go to that dance. No way, no chance, not in this lifetime."

Jess nods. "Are you sure?"

She drives me insane, but you've got to love her.

Chapter Two

The next day starts out with a double whammy of badness: first-period gym and then the dreaded French test. My stomach starts twisting as soon as the test papers get passed down the rows. The first part is multiple choice, which isn't *that* bad, but then there's a listening section. Madame Lefkowitz prowls the aisles, giving dictation with her usual mocking, I'm-sure-you-don't-know-*this* delivery. With her gray curls, eyes magnified by round black-framed glasses, and neck that seems to melt into her shoulders, she looks like an oversize owl. And if her voice in English is any clue, we're all learning how to speak French with total New Jersey accents. She calls us "Madda-mwah-ZELL" and "Muss-YOU-er."

I chew on my pencil eraser, which tastes like old glue. I studied like crazy last night, so the answers are swirling around in my head. *I* know *this*, I think every time Madame Lefkowitz dictates a question, but as soon as my pencil tip lands on the paper, the right answer seems to fly off into space. The more times this happens, of course, the more nervous I get.

At long last I hand in my paper to Madame Lefkowitz, who sniffs, "I hope it's *très* BONE this time, Madda-mwah-ZELL Donato."

You and me both, I think, crossing my fingers for luck. As I stagger out to the hall, taking deep breaths, I have to remind myself that I actually am a good student and would probably do even better if I didn't turn into a total basket case whenever I hear the word *test*.

Next up is my home and careers class. This is a big waste of time — we learn things like how to make meat loaf and balance a checkbook and the Nine Steps to Making Decisions — but the teacher is nice and I get to sit with my friends, Amelia and Sara. Amelia spends most of the class doing sudoku puzzles, but Sara takes notes on everything. She's our overachiever. She's a straight-A student, and first clarinet in the band, and on the soccer team. Last year she was regional spelling bee champion.

"Didn't we have the Seven Steps to Making Decisions in sixth-grade health?" Amelia whispers to me while Sara does her studious thing.

"Absolutely," I whisper back. "But now we've got *nine*."

"What are the extra two?"

"Seventh and eighth grade?" I offer, and we both laugh.

After class, the three of us head to lunch. Jess is already in the cafeteria, saving our favorite table (all the tables have chipped linoleum, but we like to imagine that ours is the least chipped). As usual, Jess has a PB&J made by her mother, I have the big, colorful Cobb salad I made for myself this morning, Amelia is buying the hot lunch, and Sara's unpacking take-out containers from her family's Indian restaurant. Her food smells amazing, and she's always willing to swap a samosa for a bag of Doritos or Oreos.

"How was your test?" Jess asks me as I pour dressing over my salad. Amelia comes back with a chicken patty on a bun, grayish green beans, and an extra portion of soggy french fries for the rest of us.

"Horrible. I forgot everything."

"I don't get it," says Sara. "You've got a great memory. You can memorize every line of a play — I couldn't do that. Ever."

"Yeah, but she doesn't get stage fright on stage," says Jess, grabbing one of Amelia's fries. "Only on tests."

"*C'est* VRAY," I croak in my best imitation of Madame Lefkowitz, pulling my shoulders up to my ears, and the others crack up.

I'm glad I can put my acting abilities to use in *some* way.

After lunch, my next class is English, with my favorite teacher, Mr. Amtzis. We're reading *Romeo and Juliet* now, so it's almost like having a drama class.

I start toward the classroom, nearly colliding with Will in the hall. He's carrying a long, flat instrument case.

"Sorry," he says. "Wide load."

"Is that your bass guitar?" I ask.

Will nods. "Doesn't fit in my locker. The band room is locked."

He's looking at me, and I feel like I ought to say something, but whatever I think of feels dumb. Maybe his shyness is catching.

"Oh," I say, wincing inside. In the wide world of dumb things to say, there is nothing much dumber than "Oh."

"That gig I have Saturday?" Will shuffles in place, looking awkward.

"At the Foreman Academy?"

He nods. "If you and Jess wanted to come, that would, um . . . you could do that."

"Really?" I'm completely surprised. I was positive he hadn't wanted us to come. Jess will gloat, but so what? We're invited!

"I'm allowed to bring two guests, and Ethan can't come, so . . ." He trails off, maybe realizing this sounded kind of rude.

"That's awesome!" I say as the bell rings for class. We both take a step toward the door, and I nearly run into his bass case again. Will gestures that I should go first, and I step past him into the classroom, wondering why I'm so clumsy around him. It's not as if I have a crush or anything stupid; I just think he's nice.

And maybe a little bit cute.

Jess practically screams with delight when she hears the news. "That's excellent!" she says as we walk out of school together. "I can't wait to hear Will play. *And* we get to invade the Preppy Palace!"

"Assuming that Fay lets me go. You know how she is about Saturday nights." My stepmother thinks Dad is too lenient with me, so I've learned that my chances are better if I ask her first. If I get permission from Dad in advance, she thinks we're ganging up on her and vetoes his yes every time. So I promise Jess I'll take it up with Fay when I get home tonight. Meanwhile, she'll see if her mother can give us a ride.

I get Jess's text message as soon as I finish my shift at the cleaners:

yes on sat nite ride!!! cn u come? tell me asap

I text back a quick **ok**, and picture Jess reading it on her beloved red phone. *My* cell is a dull once-silver, now gray castoff from Fay's office, with no style at all. Jess's holds four hundred songs and takes really good photos. I want one just like it, but in purple. I stick my phone into my backpack, shut my locker, and head up to the front of the cleaners to meet Dad.

He's always the last person to leave the building, and I usually wait on the customer bench near the candy machines while he goes through his closing routine. It feels good to sit down after pushing a cart back and forth for three hours and hanging up hundreds of garments.

Sometimes I'll wander, just looking around. The workroom feels totally different after the cleaning machines are shut down for the night. The plastic-bagged clothes hanging from the conveyor belt always remind me of ghosts. There's a kind of spooky hush in the air, as if they might come back to life any minute. As if magic could happen.

But today I'm anxious to go home and talk to Fay, so of course Dad is taking forever. There's a bald man inside the office with him and they're talking business. I sit on the bench, digging through my book bag for my iPod. Before I put in the earbuds, I lean toward the door to see if there's any chance they might be done soon. At first I can't hear what they're saying, but Dad's voice gets louder and more agitated.

"I can't do that, Morris. I can't," Dad says. The other man mumbles something, and Dad asks, "Well, what if I didn't replace the part-timer who's going on leave?"

My heart jumps. That must be Elise, who starts basketball practice in less than two weeks.

"That won't cut it," the other man says. "It'd have to be someone full-time."

Is this guy saying Dad has to fire someone? Even through the closed door, I can hear Dad let out a long sigh. The other man says, "There's three tailors on staff. Could you —"

Dad cuts him off. "Not Loretta or Sadie. When my father retired, I promised him they would have jobs for life."

"How about Martinez?"

I sit bolt upright. Dad can't fire Nelson! He can't!

There's a long pause, and I hold my breath. Finally, Dad says, "I'm not going to put someone's job on the block."

"Then you've got to raise prices, Frank. Something's got to give."

"You've said your piece, Morris. I've heard you." I hear Dad's chair scraping the floor as he stands and says, "Thank you."

I scramble to put in my earbuds as two sets of footsteps come toward the office door. Dad opens it wide and breaks into his usual grin. "There she is! You remember my daughter, Diana?"

"You were *this* high," says the bald man, holding a hand to his hip. I force my lips into a smile, take the earbuds back out, and say, "Hi."

"Time flies like a jumbo jet. Mine are in college already." Morris shakes his head. "We'll be in touch, okay? *Ciao.*" He heads for the front door, and Dad follows him.

"Wait up, it's already locked." Dad hauls out his key ring and opens the door. When he turns back to look at me, his face is completely calm. "I'm sorry that took me so long. You probably don't remember him, but Morris is my accountant, and we're doing my quarterly taxes. I should have let Cat drop you off after work. Did you get some of your homework done anyway?" He's switching off lights as he speaks.

I can't believe he's so cheerful. I'm dying to ask about Nelson — he *can't* lose his job; he needs every penny for grad school! — but there's no way I'm going to let on I was listening, so I go along with his mood. It's a real acting challenge. My mom was the one who loved going to plays, but watching my dad hum and putter his way through his closing routine, as if he didn't have a care in the world, I wonder if he might be more of an actor than I ever realized.

"There!" he says. "Done. After you, madame."

"Mademoiselle," I correct him, with a small smile, and he tips an invisible hat, holding the door open as I pass. I have such an urge to wrap my arms around him and hug him the way I did when I was little, but I don't want him wondering why I'm suddenly so sentimental. He sets the burglar alarm and follows me out to the parking lot.

• • •

"What took you so long?" is how Fay says hello when we get home. She has what my grandpapa would call "an unfortunate manner." Not for the first time, I wonder if Papa and Nonni retired to Florida not because they were tired of running the cleaners, but because Dad got married to Fay. They practically moved in with us after Mom died, and I think getting used to Fay and her daughters just broke their hearts. It didn't do much for mine either. I still think of Mom every day, and I always will.

Fay is still dressed as a real estate broker, in a cream-colored pantsuit and gold button earrings, with her frosted blond hair as stiff as a bicycle helmet. I wonder why she hasn't changed; she gets off work at three, when my step-sisters come home from elementary school. "The table needs setting," she says briskly, plunking a bag of peas into the microwave.

This means me, of course, though I'm still in my corduroy jacket and scarf, and the twins are just sitting there. Ashley is watching TV in the living room, and Brynna is hunched at the dining table. She's working on some kind of school project, making a covered wagon out of a shoe box. "That looks really nice," I tell her, and Brynna pouts and says, "Ashley's is better."

I look into a box on the end table, where Ashley has made a small scene with a mini American Girl doll and several My Little Ponys on plastic grass. It must have taken her all of five minutes.

I help Brynna carry her art supplies into the living room, then go back to the kitchen for place settings. "Something smells good," I say. I'm determined to be as pleasant as possible, for two reasons: I have a favor to ask, and I promised my dad I'd be nicer to Fay.

Dinner tonight is a rotisserie chicken from the Price Chopper, lentil pilaf, and peas, with white rice for the twins, who are iffy on pilaf. They're in third grade, where the rule of thumb seems to be Don't Eat Any Food You Can't Spell.

While we eat, I keep looking at Dad, who shows no signs of stress as he talks to the twins about westward expansion and class dioramas. He suggests that Brynna cut up some cheesecloth to cover her wagon. "It's got the right drape," he says. "Better than paper."

I wonder if he'll talk to Fay later tonight about what his accountant said. She's a smart businesswoman, and he often asks her advice. If she tells him to let Nelson go, I'll never forgive her. I look at her manicured hands as she cuts little pieces of chicken, reminding myself of the Be Nice to Fay Project.

I clear all the dishes without being asked, bring dessert to the table, and clear those plates, too. Fay is brewing a fresh pot of decaf as I load the dishwasher. *It's now or never*, I think, looking over at her.

"Can I go to a dance with Jess Saturday night?" I blurt. "Her mother can drive us."

"Where?" she says, frowning.

"The Foreman Academy."

Fay's eyebrows lift. "Who do *you* know at the Foreman Academy?" Her tone is accusing, as if I've been secretly making upscale friends behind her back.

"Nobody. One of my classmates is in the band," I explain.

"We've got plans for this weekend."

First I've heard about it. This is where I need some

strategy. She's teetering over the edge of no, and if I push at all, she'll fall in and stay there. I take a deep breath, counting to ten on the exhale, the way our drama coach taught us.

"What plans?" asks my father. I wince. Now she'll think we're in this together.

Sure enough, Fay shoots him a look. "Don't take a tone with me, Frank. I have things to get done, and I need Diana to stay with the girls."

Dad doesn't flinch. He says in his most soothing voice, "I'm planning to be at home Saturday night. But I'll tell you what. We've got definite plans for *next* Saturday night, and I think Diana could sit for us then. Am I right?"

I nod vigorously. Fay is frowning. "Every time. It's like clockwork. You take her side against mine, and I get —"

"Get what?" says Dad, slipping his arms around her. "A free babysitter for our anniversary?" Fay looks at him, her expression softening.

"I already made reservations," Dad says. "I'm not telling you where. But I think this should work out quite nicely for all my girls."

Fay and I look at each other, not thrilled, but accepting the compromise. Ashley pipes up, "You mean we have to stay with *her*?"

When the last pot is washed, I go up to my bedroom. It's next to the attic and has the same low-slanting ceiling. I have one wall covered with a giant collage of old Playbills and posters, and there's my Accessory Wall, with rows of large and small hooks for all my necklaces, belts, scarves, and hats. The room's not very big, but it's full of the things I love most, and I always feel happy when I step inside. It's my sanctuary.

I turn on my laptop and log onto my e-mail. There's a message from Jess that says, "Check this out!" with a link to the Foreman Academy Web site. I open it up right away.

The campus sits high on the Palisades, the cliffs over-looking the Hudson River. Jess is right: I've driven past its tall gates many times, but the buildings are far away from the road, so this is the first time I've actually gotten a look at the campus. It looks like Hogwarts crossed with a Gothic cathedral: towers, stone arches, ivy. It's hard to believe kids actually go to a posh-looking school like this, only a few miles away. And we're going to be there on Saturday!

I browse through the gallery. The grounds are as green as a golf course, and the students all look like models. The uniforms are totally old-school: navy blue blazers with crests, over gray flannel pants for the boys and plaid skirts for the girls. I'm starting to get into the fantasy, when I spot a photograph of the school's brand-new theatre, state-of-the-art and enormous. My heart fills with envy. It looks like a real Broadway stage!

I flop down on my bed and call Jess. She answers halfway through the first ring. "So? Can you go?"

I say yes and instantly move the phone two feet away from my ear, since I'm so sure she'll scream. Which she does. "I can't believe this!" she says. "Did you check out the Web site? This place is insane!"

"Did you see their theatre? I wish we went to school there!"

"Cut me a break, fashionista," says Jess. "You'd hate going to a school that has uniforms."

"*Our* school has uniforms. Kayleigh Carell Mall Rat, Football Jock Casual, Skateboader Emo . . ."

"Good point. But it isn't *official*."

A stray thought flies into my head. "You don't think they have to wear blazers and skirts to the dance?"

"I hope not," says Jess. "We'll stand out like sore thumbs."

"What are *we* going to wear?" I say, casting a critical eye over the Accessory Wall. I love everything on it, but nothing screams out "prep school dance."

"Well, *you've* got the Nelson Couture gown he made you for *Angel*."

"No, I don't. I gave it back to him for his grad school portfolio." And then I can't help it. I turn up my iTunes for privacy and pour out the whole conversation I overheard today between my dad and his accountant, about Nelson's job being in danger. Jess is as upset as I am.

"That's awful, Diana."

"Dad can't fire Nelson. I'll quit." That wouldn't do much good, since I'm not an official employee — I did get a bump in my weekly allowance, but I'm not on the payroll. For the first time, I realize that my job isn't just about Fay thinking I'm old enough to pitch in: I'm saving my father a part-timer's salary.

I glance at my laptop. The lush green lawns of the Foreman Academy look more inviting than ever.

Saturday finally comes, and even though Fay loads me down with a huge list of chores, and the twins keep on picking ridiculous fights with each other, I'm too excited to care. I've tried on every piece of my wardrobe five times, and narrowed it down to six choices, more or less. I put everything into my duffel bag, then add three pairs of shoes (just in case) and a generous sampling of jewelry and scarves. When I come downstairs with the bulging bag over my shoulder, Dad bursts out laughing.

"You look like you're going to some other country."

I am. Land of the Preps.

Jess has done exactly the same thing, and her bedroom is covered with outfits. Her room is no bigger than mine, and it's just as colorful, though the theme is more Jonas Brothers than theatre and fashion. Nick is her favorite; she even has posters of him on the ceiling. She cranks up the music and we try on everything in my duffel and off the top of her bed, mixing and matching, sending things over the top with her Mad Hatter top hat, or my unmatched striped socks, or her tutu, or all three at once. We snap endless pictures on Jess's cell phone, and we laugh so hard, both of us actually hurt.

Finally we settle on outfits we're willing to wear out in public. Jess puts on a forest green dress that sets off her red hair, with a black angora cardigan I found in my favorite vintage boutique, and strappy black shoes with a cute little heel. I'm wearing a turquoise patterned dress with a great swirly skirt and purple ballet flats. My hair is clipped back on one side with a rhinestone barrette I wore in *My Fair Lady*. We look at ourselves in the big bathroom mirror, and each thinks the other looks great.

As we stand side by side trading compliments — "You look *so* cute," "No, *you* look cute" — Jess's kid brother, Dash, heads down the hall, takes one look through the open door, and says, "No contest. You both look disgusting."

"Get lost!" shouts Jess. She lunges at him as he runs for the stairs.

"Bet you can't run in those shoes!"

"Mo-om! Dash is being a jerk!"

"Leave each other alone." Mrs. Munson's voice wafts upstairs, sounding really tired, like she's been through this one too many times.

Dash is in the front seat of the Munsons' old Subaru wagon. Mrs. Munson is dropping him off at a friend's, where they're going to watch *Transformers*, again, and pretend that they're blowing things up.

"What are you going to do with two hours on your own, Mom?" asks Jess as we pull away from Dash's friend's house.

"Sleep," says Mrs. Munson, who works double shifts every Friday. She makes the word sound like the best thing on earth.

The Foreman Academy isn't that far from our houses, but the drive is exciting. The road hugs the cliffs, with a view of the Manhattan skyline just over the river. The Empire State Building is lit up in blue, and the two swoops of cable that run the length of the George Washington Bridge are sparkling with spotlights, like giant-size necklaces.

Everything glitters: the city, the bridge, even the lights on the planes overhead.

Finally we get to a cast-iron fence that stretches along wooded grounds to a giant stone gate. A small brass plaque on the archway says FOREMAN ACADEMY, and there's a gatehouse with a security guard.

"Wow," says Jess under her breath as her mother pulls up to the gatehouse and rolls down a window.

No kidding.

"May I help you?" The guard's voice belongs on the radio.

Mrs. Munson says, "I'm dropping off these two girls for a dance? They should be on the guest list."

"The guest list for the *band*, Mom!" Jess hisses.

The guard looks for our names on his clipboard, turning over a page before he says, "Yes, fine. You can park in Lot B, by the gym." He waves one hand off toward the right, and we follow a long driveway onto the campus.

The academy's Web site photos were all taken on bright sunny days. At night, the buildings are lit from the bottom, so they look even grander and more overwhelming, with shadows of giant oaks falling across the ivy-covered walls.

"This is *sick*!" Jess breathes, pressing her face to the car window. "Are those buildings *dorms*? It looks like a college!"

It looks more like heaven to me. I'm completely knocked out.

"Which way is Lot B?" says her mother. "Look, there are some kids. I'll pull over and ask them."

"NO!" Jess and I say in unison. These students *live* here. Bad enough that we're getting dropped off, but a parent asking for directions is beyond embarrassing. "Just drive the same way that they're heading."

I look out the window. The students I see — two tall blond girls and two dark-eyebrowed boys — are an eerie matched set, all perfectly dressed and well groomed in their dark coats. It's like *Gossip Girl* live.

Jess and I look at each other. "Can you spell *attitude*?" she says.

"Oh, come on, they're just preps. What did you expect?"

"I bet they're all stuck-up snobs."

"So what?" I say, trying to sound like I mean it. "We're just here to dance."

44

"Right. And hear Will."

Mrs. Munson pulls into a parking space next to a building that's probably the gym. The four well-dressed students are heading right for it, and even through the car windows, I can hear amplified music coming from inside. Will's band must be playing! Weirdly, this makes me feel even more nervous.

"I'll pick you up right here at ten P.M. Have you got your phone?" asks Mrs. Munson. Jess nods and we both thank her mother for driving. Then we get out of the old station wagon and stand side by side, staring up at the Foreman Academy gym. This is a whole different world.

"Come on," says Jess. "Let's go watch Lifestyles of the Rich and Snooty."

Jess always makes me laugh. And at the moment that's just what I need.

Chapter Three

Jess and I do our best to look poised — we are both actresses, after all, so we know how to make a good entrance — but both of us let out a gasp when we enter the Foreman gymnasium. Our middle school's gym is a scuffed-up addition with battered pine floors, folding bleachers, and lightbulbs in cages so they won't get clobbered by basketballs.

This building looks so . . . *expensive.* The entrance hallway is paneled in oak, with leaded-glass windows, life-size portraits of former headmasters, group photos of teams, and a glass-fronted case full of trophy cups.

I give Jess a nudge. "What do you think those trophies are for? Polo?"

"NASCAR racing and paintball."

"Be good," I say, giggling.

The doors at the end of the hall are wide open. The band's onstage, playing a cover of Pink's "So What." It's upbeat and fun and the lead vocalist can really sing. I'm eager to see Will on the bandstand.

"Come on," I say, grabbing Jess by the hand.

The gym is enormous, decked out with giant balloons in the school colors, royal blue and gold. The stage is right in the middle, along the back wall, and there's Will on the left with an electric bass strapped over one shoulder.

He looks like a rocker. The gangling, not-sure-what-to-do-with-myself shyness he has at school is totally gone onstage: Maybe all he needs is an instrument in his hands. He sways just a bit as he plays, with his hair spilling over his forehead, and when he leans in toward the mike to do harmony vocals, I'm so proud of him that I feel the tips of my ears flushing pink.

"They sound *great*!" Jess yells over the music. The singer is a slim Asian girl with long glossy hair and a great pair of red lace-up boots. She's playing a bright blue acoustic guitar. The lead guitar must be Will's brother, Steve — his hair's short and straight, but when he and Will lean in to sing backup, their faces are almost identical. The drummer is compact and wiry, with wavy blond hair and a habit of biting his lip as he plays. They might be a high school band, but I'd buy their CD for sure. No wonder Will was so psyched by this chance.

Just like the dances at our school there are more clumps of boys and girls dancing together than actual couples. This is a good thing, since no one will think it's weird if Jess and I just dance with each other. We're both feeling too out of place to jump into the pack.

We bop around to the music for the rest of the song, then cheer and clap with everyone else. Will grins and surveys the crowd, squinting into the lights. Am I imagining it, or is he looking for us?

"Want to go and say hi?" says Jess.

"Let's check out the snacks first."

Jess nods enthusiastically. Along the side wall are two tables covered with white cloths, each holding big crystal bowls full of fruit punch and platters of snacks: butter cookies, biscotti, a tropical fruit platter, chips, and fresh guacamole — even the junk food looks expensive. Not for the first time, I wonder: *What would it be like to go to a school like this?*

Jess picks up a spear of fresh pineapple. "If this is what they serve at dances, imagine the lunch."

"Imagine the budget for their school plays!" Our drama club barely limps from one show to another. We're always repainting the same flimsy wall flats, and have to hold bake sales whenever we need to build platforms or rent real costumes. The thought of going to a school where this wouldn't be an issue, where they probably have theatre *classes*, not just an edited Shakespeare play in your English class every two years, is mouthwatering. I feel the same way I did when I saw the movie *Fame*, about the performing arts high school in New York City: If going to school was like *that*, not all math worksheets and French tests, I'd love every minute. The Foreman Academy looks like a paradise.

Jess ladles out two cups of fruit punch, and we find a good vantage point three or four rows up the bleachers to check out the scene. The band's playing "Dirty Little Secret" by the All-American Rejects, and Steve takes the lead vocal. The girl singer stands so close to him at the mike that I wonder if they might be boyfriend and girlfriend offstage. They *look* like a couple, but you never know. When I saw Adam Kessler walk into the opening night party with his costar, I assumed the same thing but was thrilled to find out I was wrong. The whole couple thing is a total mystery to me. I've had crushes on celebrities, but the only time I've crushed on someone I've actually met was with Adam, who *was* my celebrity crush, so I don't think that counts.

Jess leans in closer. "Is it just me, or are *all* these boys cute?" she whispers into my ear. "I mean, what are the odds? Think about it. Our school has eight hundred students — that's four hundred boys, more or less — and maybe three of them aren't revolting. It's so unfair."

I follow her gaze. In a way, I realize that the Foreman Academy is kind of like Weehawken Middle School on steroids. The cute boys seem even cuter, the weird chaperones even weirder, and the mean girls even meaner — I notice the tall blond pair that we saw outside taunting two younger girls, who look like they're ready to cry.

"OMG! Check out that boy over there," Jess says.

"Where?"

"By the food table. Black V-neck sweater and cargos. He looks like Nick Jonas!"

"Black V-neck . . ." I'm not spotting him.

"Curly hair, laughing. He's dipping a Terra chip into the guacamole."

"Oh, yeah. He is kind of cute."

"Kind of? He's *gorgeous*! Look at those dimples." Jess points at him just as he looks our way. She covers her face with her hands. "Oh my god. I'm going to die of embarrassment. Is he still looking?"

"He waved at you."

"What?" Jess tears her hands off her face and looks back, but the boy's turned away, saying something to one of his friends. "He's making a joke about me. I can tell. Did he really wave?"

"Yes, Jess, he really did." She looks back at the boy, and I realize that the two tall blond girls are staring right at us and frowning. I think we've been pegged as crashers. My stomach drops. The last thing I want is a couple of millionaire Kayleigh Carells picking on us. "Don't look now, but we're being stared at."

51

"What?" Jess whips her head around, which is always exactly what happens when you tell someone not to look now.

"It's those two girls we saw coming in. Blonde and Blonder. Let's get out of their way for a while. Did you see a bathroom anywhere?"

"There was one in the hall. Good idea." We climb down from the bleachers as inconspicuously as we can — not very — and head for the hall with our punch cups.

The bathroom is spotless, with white marble tiles. No scratched-in hearts with initials, no Sharpied graffiti, no wadded paper towels all over the floor. There's a big mirror lit by sconces, and even the sinks have gold fixtures.

"Jess. This is a *school* bathroom. Inside a *gym*."

"I know, right? It's insane. Is there anyone in here?"

I look under the stall doors for shoes. "Nope, just us."

"Good." Jess whips out her cell phone, puts an arm over my shoulder, and snaps a quick photo of us in the mirror. "No one would believe this unless we have evidence." As she takes a second shot, the door opens wide and the two blond girls stroll in.

Great. Nothing embarrassing about getting caught taking photographs of a school bathroom.

The taller blonde leans toward the mirror, retouching her flawless mascara. She has a shell-pink French manicure that matches her headband, and earrings that match her gold choker. Her sheath dress is ivory silk.

I make a big show of washing my hands as Jess hastily stuffs her phone into her hobo bag, zipping it tight. The second blonde, in a sky blue plaid halter dress, eyes the bag disdainfully.

"Someone's been shopping at Salvation Army," she says, snapping open her Kate Spade clutch and applying a spritz of perfume to her neck. "Want some, Brooke?"

Brooke doesn't bother to answer. *Wow*, I think, *she even gives attitude to her friends*.

"Do you two go to this school?" Brooke asks. It isn't really a question; she already knows. My heart stops for a nanosecond as she meets my eye in the mirror.

"Um, no. We have friends in the band."

I'm hoping this makes us sound cool, but she looks me over, barrette to ballet flats. "I *told* you they're locals," she says to her friend, turning back to the mirror as if we're not there.

"Could you believe that? I wanted to yank her hair! Kayleigh and Savannah times twenty," Jess huffs as we go back into the gym.

"They're always blond. Why are they always blond? *I* wouldn't act like that if I was blond."

"Amelia doesn't act like that. Or that girl at the cleaners, Elise. It isn't the hair, it's the attitude. Oh, help, there's Nick Jonas again." Jess's hand flies up to her mouth as the boy in the black V-neck leaves his friends and comes over.

"Hi," he says, smiling at both of us, but looking at Jess. His dimples are on full display. "Could you settle an argument?"

"Sure," Jess squeaks out in about half her voice.

"What were you pointing at before?"

Jess blushes bright red and just stammers. "I . . . I . . ."

I come to her rescue. "Terra chip. Sweet potato's her favorite."

"Mine, too," he says, grinning. "My friend said it was the tag of my shirt sticking up, so I just won five bucks. I'm Jason."

Jess somehow recovers her voice. "I'm Jess, and this is Diana. We're friends of the band."

"Cool!" Jason says. "They're really good. Would you want to try dancing to them?" His eyes are on Jess. It's as if he's forgotten I'm standing right there. I shift from one foot to the other. I'm not exactly *jealous*, but I can't help but feel a little left out.

"Um, sure," says Jess, looking at me. I can't tell if she's checking to see if I'm cool with her leaving, or wants me to join them.

I definitely don't want to be a third wheel, so I say, "Maybe later. My foot kind of hurts." This turns out to be the right answer, since Jess beams at me, shoving her hobo bag into my hands. "Keep this safe, okay? Thanks!" she says, and disappears into the crowd with Jason.

I sigh. I don't know anyone else in the room except

Will, and he's kind of busy right now. Also, I don't want to be standing right by the door when Brooke and her sidekick return from the bathroom.

I walk back past the food table, stopping to scoop up some french onion dip with a Terra chip. Jason and Jess are dancing with some of his friends, but he's looking at her more than anywhere else. He's an energetic, slightly goofy dancer, flailing his arms and grinning a lot. Jess is glowing as if she just met her own Adam Kessler, except that he isn't a celebrity and he is the right age for her. *Not fair*, I think with a stab of envy. And then I feel guilty that I'm not being a better friend. I should be excited for Jess. Neither of us has had anything close to a boyfriend before. This is huge.

All of a sudden I realize I've got her purse, with her cell phone inside. She'd die if she saw me take pictures of her, but I bet I could sneak a few. *She'll want them afterward*, I tell myself. Just like the ritzy school bathroom, it's evidence.

Now I've got a mission. I take out the phone, being careful to hide its red case inside my cupped hand as I work my way into the crowd. When I get close enough to Jason and Jess, I pretend to adjust the barrette in my hair, and fire off four quick shots of Jason over Jess's shoulder. Then I circle around to the other side.

This is harder, because Jess is smiling right at me, signaling that I should join Jason's friends. I come closer, not really quite *dancing*, but bopping in place to the music the way someone with a sore foot might. When Jess turns toward Jason, I sneak two more shots from waist level, hoping they're both in the frame.

The band ends the song, and the crowd cheers. I can't resist snapping a shot of Jess cupping her hands around her mouth and cheering loudly as Jason lets loose with a two-fingered whistle.

The girl singer says, "Thanks so much!" She turns to Will's brother, who leans toward the mike and says, "This song is older than we are, but it's still a goodie. Will?"

Will nods and starts playing the bass line of the B-52s' "Rock Lobster," a favorite oldie at drama club parties. Jason and Jess immediately launch into fish-inspired dance moves, cracking each other up. This is a definite photo op. I spy-cam them doing the swim, blowing fake bubbles — plus a truly terrible one of Jason holding his nose next to a puffy-cheeked Jess as the band sings, "Down . . . down . . . down."

Too funny! Jess will go nuts when she sees that one, just like I did when she took those photos of me in my work smock. But this is why DELETE buttons exist. I'll show it to her, let her shriek, then I'll delete it.

Satisfied, I walk back toward the bandstand and can't resist snapping one more of Will strumming his bass. Just as I shoot, he turns his head toward me. I have to think fast. Slipping the phone back into Jess's bag, I pretend I've come over to leave our purses next to the stage so I can dance. I walk past the speakers and set both the bags down on the floor near the instrument cases.

With my hands now free, I start back toward Jess and Jason, but stop when I notice the two blond girls again. The taller one, Brooke, is glaring right at Jess, her eyes narrowing. *What did she do to you?* I think. *Leave her alone!*

And then I get it. Brooke must like Jason! It's hard to imagine that he likes Brooke back — he seems pretty down-to-earth for a prep — but he *is* really cute. I guess even mean girls get jealous.

This thought makes me happier than I can say.

Everyone cheers when the band finishes "Rock Lobster." Steve grins, introducing the band members one by one, and there's a swell of applause after every one. Will's last, and even though I'm cheering, too, I can hear Jess's "WOO-HOO!" from across the room.

"We're gonna take a short break," Steve says. "Hey, Adam, hit the iPod mix, okay? Don't stop dancing now, we'll be back in fifteen." The drummer flips a switch, and Vampire Weekend blares through the speakers. The band members turn away from the crowd, chatting and unplugging their instruments. Will's big brother high-fives him. Will grins, sets his bass down, and jumps off the stage, making his way right to me.

I can feel myself smiling too wide, and I overhear a Foreman girl's pouty "I should've known he was taken." This catches me off guard — I didn't expect *Will* to be crush bait. (And she thought *we* were a couple? Too funny!) But he's too stoked up from nerves and adrenaline to notice his fan.

"Whoa," he says. "That was *intense*. I just learned that song yesterday."

"No way!"

"Steve wanted to skip it, but I made him promise to let me try." He pulls at the neck of his T-shirt. "Is it just me, or is it a hundred degrees in here?"

"Stage lights," I say. "Let's go stand by the door."

"Sure, yeah." Will's looking around in a distracted haze, a feeling I recognize from the intermissions of plays I've been in. You're energized and exhausted at the same time, and you know you've still got Act Two to get through.

Someone's propped open the side door behind the stage, and there's a nice breeze. We stand right beside the door, and Will reaches into a cooler the band brought and hands me an ice-cold Coke. "Steve and I had a band at our old school in Santa Fe. When we moved east, I figured we'd start another. But he met Sou Mei, and her band's got a dynamite bass player, I mean when his fingers aren't broken, so . . . anyway." He flips open his soda can and takes a gulp.

I drink from mine, too. "What do you think of this school?" I ask.

Will looks out at the weird shadows on the quad and stone clock tower. "Good place to shoot monster movies."

"Night of the Living Snobs," says Jason, who comes up behind us, with Jess at his side.

"That was *great*!" she says, giving Will a high five. "Will, this is Jason. He goes to school here."

"Don't rub it in," Jason says. "Hey, your band really rocks."

"Thanks." Apparently, Will has retreated back into his shy mode.

Jason says, "I'm taking Jess on a tour of the campus. You guys want to come?"

I actually don't, but I can tell Jess wants my company this time around. Being totally one-on-one with a brand-new crush would make me nervous, too. I'd probably forget how to talk.

"Sure," I say, glancing at Will and hoping he'll join us.

He shuffles his feet, looking down at the ground. "I better not. Got to go over the second set list, and . . . yeah.

You know. Tune up and stuff." He's all the way back to his English class mumble, and I can't help smiling.

"Later," I say, and we head outside.

Jason's a lively and talkative tour guide. He points out the boys' and girls' dorms, which look like fancy hotels with their rows of lit windows. Then he shows us the quad with the clock tower, main classroom building, library, and dining hall — "Note, that is *not* a 'cafeteria.' That would be *common*."

I know what I want to see most. "Where's the theatre?" I ask. Jess's ears perk up, too.

"Follow me," Jason says. He leads us behind the library, toward a modern white building that looks like it could've migrated from Lincoln Center. There's a tall metal sculpture in front with mobile pieces that drift in the breeze. "Witness the Abercrombie Arts Center."

"Abercrombie, as in — ?"

He nods. "Sweatshirts with moose. Some relative is an alumnus who signed a big check, even by Foreman Academy standards. It's probably locked, but you never know. Some dance hater might be inside doing late-night ceramics."

"Ceramics!" I'm practically drooling. I'd love to try using a potter's wheel. Imagine these kids having that in their art room!

Jason tries the front door, but it's locked tight. So's the studio entrance and the backstage loading dock. He looks irritated. "I'm going to call campus security. Tell them I left something inside the building." He pulls out an iPhone.

"It's fine," says Jess. "Really."

Jason holds up a hand as someone picks up on the other end. "Yes, hi. Jason Geissinger here. I need to get into the Abercrombie Center. I left my trumpet inside a practice room, and someone locked up. . . . Yes, I'll wait." He hangs up.

"You play trumpet?" Jess asks.

"No." Jason grins. "What do they know? He'll be here in five." He's a little bit cocky for my taste, but Jess laughs as if that's the funniest thing she's ever heard. As we stand around, waiting for the security guard, Jason tells us about himself, how his dad is a coffee importer and travels all over the world. "That's why I got stuck at this dump," he says.

Dump seems an odd choice of word for a school with a full-service arts complex. They even have animation and filmmaking classes, according to Jason. I can't imagine a school where I'd get to take theatre and film and ceramics for credit. "Do you guys have home and careers?" I ask.

Jason looks blank. "What's that?"

Yes! It's official: This place is too good to be true.

The security guard finally shows up and lets us all inside. It occurs to me that he must think Jess and I go here, and that makes me almost as happy as getting to see that incredible stage. Jason fumbles with worklights, and we go out onto the huge, polished stage. For fun, I begin to quote a few lines I remember from *Romeo and Juliet*, and Jason surprises us both by saying a line from the balcony scene.

"Do you act?" Jess says breathlessly.

"Nope." He grins. "Only in English class."

"We're doing *Romeo and Juliet*, too!" I exclaim, and suddenly realize our being here is a lot like the play. The dance in the gym is the Capulets' ball, and Jess and I are the outsider Montagues, sneaking into a party where we don't belong.

By the time we get back to the quad, the clock on the

tower says 9:55. Jess's eyes widen. "My mom's probably already waiting for us." Then she turns and looks at me. "Where's my bag?"

"Oh." I gulp with a sudden realization. "I left it inside by the stage."

"You *what*?" She looks horrified.

"It's right next to mine. I'll go get them," I say, and speed up, feeling guilty. The truth is I just plain forgot about leaving our bags. I can hear the band's music from inside the gym, and I pick up my pace. I dart in through the side door and grab our two purses, waving a hasty goodbye to Will. He's playing, but he dips the neck of his bass up and down as if he's waving back.

I dodge through the crowd, being sure to avoid Blonde and Blonder, and race down the hall past the portraits and trophy case, coming out the front door. I see a boy and girl under a streetlight ahead, standing next to the parking lot. It's funny how even a small heel can change someone's posture — if it weren't for the red hair, I'd think that was some older girl. But no, it's just Jess and Jason, probably feeling awkward now that they're alone, and probably a little giddy, too. *Should I join them or not?*

The decision's made for me as Mrs. Munson's old Subaru lumbers up the long driveway. I trot over and hand Jess her purse as her mother pulls up.

"Bye," she says breathlessly, turning toward Jason.

"I'll call you tomorrow," he says with a dimply smile, patting his iPhone. "Got your number right here. Bye, Diana. Nice meeting you. Bye, Jess."

He waves, and walks back toward the gym, turning twice as we're getting into the car. He looks as smitten as Jess does. I can't believe it! Did Jess just find an almost-boyfriend?

"Who was that?" asks Mrs. Munson.

"Just some boy," Jess says in the world's worst imitation of couldn't-care-less.

"Okay," says her mother, amused. She backs out of the space and heads toward the gatehouse, past a neatly trimmed hedge and a long row of streetlights.

In the backseat, Jess turns and mouths at me, "I'll call you tomorrow." Even in the half dark, I can see her eyes shining.

Chapter Four

Dad and I are at our favorite bakery, picking up Sunday brunch pastries, when I get a call from Jess's home phone number. Leaving Dad to decide between the pecan rolls and cherry-cheese Danish, I take my phone into a corner. This should be pretty good gossip. I'm smiling just thinking about it.

"So? Tell me all."

"Do you have my phone?" Jess sounds frantic.

"What?"

"My cell phone. It's not in my bag. Did you put it in yours?"

"Why would I do that?"

"Check anyway."

I know it's not there, but I dig through my bag. "Nope."

"Oh, God! I bet it fell out when you picked up my bag from the gym."

I feel a sudden lurch in my stomach. Did I re-zip the front pocket after I used her phone to take pictures? I must have. I know how much Jess loves that phone.

"It didn't fall out. I'm sure I would have noticed."

"Then where is it?"

"I don't know." I feel almost as frantic as Jess. "Did you check the backseat of the car?"

"Duh! Of *course*!"

"Well, the Foreman Academy must have a lost and found."

"I already called campus security. Nobody's turned it in. What if Jason *calls* me and thinks I'm not answering?" Her voice sounds more and more desperate.

"Call Jason and tell him what happened."

"I don't have his number!" Jess practically shouts. "And the student directory doesn't list cell phones. I can't call his *parents*!"

Oh, God. This is awful.

"If you lost my phone . . ." says Jess, letting it dangle.

"I didn't. I swear, it was right in your bag." Which I left on the floor. And hope I zipped up. I don't know what to tell her, and anyway, Dad's at my elbow with two pastry boxes and the Sunday papers. "I'll come over as soon as I can. Right after brunch, okay?"

Jess doesn't answer. Her silence is terrible.

Sunday brunch at my house is a three-course affair. On top of our pastry tradition, Dad loves making things like frittatas and Canadian bacon and fruit smoothies. He says since Fay makes dinner during the week, it's his turn to do something nice for his family. So of course there's no question of rushing the process, which also includes reading Sunday funnies with Ashley and Brynna.

And since it's Fay's day of rest, I'm the one who has to help Dad clean the kitchen. It's well past noon by the time I get to Jess's house. Dash has two of his friends over, and they're making so much noise on the Xbox that Jess is completely on edge. We decide to go out for a walk.

The sky is a brilliant bright blue, and there's a sweet

charcoal smell of leaves burning in somebody's yard. Jess immediately launches into her cell phone panic.

"Did you take it out of the bag? Did you use it?" she demands.

I hesitate. The answer to both of these questions is yes, but I don't want to fan the flames by telling her I took those photos. I decide "Did you use it?" means as a *phone*, and since I didn't make any calls, it's not quite a lie when I tell her I didn't.

But it's not really the truth either. I've done enough stretching of facts to know there's a difference, and though I feel guilty, I just couldn't bear it if Jess blamed me more than she already does. So I change the subject to something I know she'll be eager to talk about: Jason.

His name does the trick. Her whole face brightens as she reports everything he said to her while they were dancing, or while they drank punch and ate Terra chips. "Sweet potato," she grins at me. "Thanks for the save, by the way."

I feel even worse about sort-of lying.

As we walk, Jess babbles nonstop about Jason and all the vacations his family has taken to places like Kenya,

Brazil, and Jamaica. We wind up at our old elementary school playground, where we sit on swings that are now much too short for our legs, watching a couple of younger kids poke through the sandbox while their mother sits on a purple bench, knitting.

"Why do you think he puts Foreman Academy down so much?" I ask, remembering Jason on the tour last night. "I would go there in a heartbeat!"

"Maybe it isn't the school," says Jess. "Maybe he just misses living at home."

Before I can ask where he lives, I feel my phone vibrating inside my pocket. "Hold on," I say, taking it out.

"Who is it?" asks Jess as I stare at the screen.

"It's *you*." We look at each other. "You texted me."

"What? That's impossible!"

I hold up my phone. On the display screen is Jess's number and:

U R SUCH A LOSER

Jess's eyes widen. "I never —"

"I know," I say.

71

"OMG." Jess turns pale. "Somebody stole my phone —
and they're pranking me!"

Jess is beyond upset. I do my best to calm her down, but
nothing helps. I even suggest that she call the phone company and have the account cancelled, and she turns on me
in a fury.

"Are you kidding? Do you know how much my mom
spent on that phone? She'll go out of her mind if I tell her
somebody lost it."

I know whom she means by "somebody": me. There's
no way I can tell her the truth now, in the state she's in. If
I confess that I took out her phone to take pictures, she'd
never forgive me. And anyway, I'm *positive* I zipped it back
into that pocket!

Or did I? I keep trying to retrace my steps and remember, but the truth is that the cell phone theft is really my
fault either way. Whether the pocket was open or closed,
I'm the one who left Jess's bag on the floor of the gym when
she told me to watch it for her. I feel like my stomach is
tied up in knots.

• • •

At school the next morning, things get even worse. When we catch up with Amelia and Sara crossing the parking lot from their bus to the door, they're both glaring at Jess.

"I'll tell you who's a loser," Amelia says angrily. "People who send rude texts."

"Yeah, right. What was up with that?" Sara says.

"You got them, too?" Jess looks stricken. "Guys, I didn't send those, I swear. I lost my phone Saturday night, and whoever found it must be texting my whole contact list. I'm going to die."

"No, you're not," I say soothingly. "We'll just spread the word that the texts aren't from you."

"Who would *do* that?" Jess wails.

"It isn't the end of the world," says Amelia.

"Easy for you to say. It's not *your* friends who hate you."

"Come on, Jess," Sara says. "We all love and adore you." She hooks her arm through Jess's and we go through the door.

The first people we see in the hall are Ethan and Kayleigh. "Who are you calling a loser, loser?" says Ethan, as Kayleigh smirks. Jess has to explain the whole thing all over again, and we have to calm her down again. The result is that we're all late to our homerooms.

First-period gym is as boring as ever. After class, as we're changing back into our school clothes, I think about telling Amelia the rest of the story, but I'm pretty sure she'll insist I tell Jess. I try to convince myself that the phone would be lost whether I speak up or not, but it's not just the phone. It's the fact that I lied to my best friend. To *Jess*.

I go into French feeling sick to my stomach. If Madame Lefkowitz hands back our tests, I might actually puke. But *non*, not today. She just makes us pair off for vocabulary drills. "Ecou-tay et repe-TAY," she squawks.

Listen and repeat. I can handle that; it's almost like acting. She makes us recite the same dialogue about ordering french fries and beefsteaks from a bistro about fifty-five times. It makes me incredibly hungry.

Next up is home and careers, where we're studying basic food groups and food pyramids. My table's assigned to the Fats, Oils, and Sweets group, and we spend the whole period cutting out magazine pictures of ice cream, chocolate, candy, and fries. This is cruel and unusual punishment.

Finally I get to lunch. Tomorrow, there's a staff-development half day, so most of the kids around us are happily making plans. But Jess is still ranting about her lost phone. "In case you haven't heard yet," she tells Will in the cafeteria line, "I *did not* text you to say you're a loser."

She takes out her wallet to pay for her milk, and he stares at her hobo bag. "Is your phone red?"

"*Yes*," she says instantly. "Why?"

"Last night, I saw a girl take a red phone out of a bag like that. Next to the bandstand."

"What did she look like?" I say, though I already know.

"Tall, blond hair, wearing a —"

Jess and I say it in unison. "Brooke."

Jess is still fuming when she walks me to the bus I take to the cleaners. "What is her *problem*? Why would you do that to someone you don't even *know*?"

"I have a theory." I tell Jess how I caught Brooke glaring at her and Jason while they were dancing together. "I think Brooke the Blonde has a crush on him."

"That is so vile. I may vomit."

Just as she says this, I feel my phone vibrate. I dig it out of my backpack and look at the screen. Sure enough, Brooke has sent a new message:

lookin' goooood!

Right underneath is a photo I took of Jess when we were trying on outfits. She's wearing a plaid flannel shirt and a tutu. Her hair is in two Pippi Longstocking braids, and her eyes are crossed.

Jess looks over my shoulder and screams so loudly that people across the parking lot turn to stare at her. "That's *horrible*!"

Not much use arguing with her. It really is.

"Diana! I can't believe you didn't delete that! Why did you have to take so many pictures?" Jess wails. "*Why* did you leave my purse where she could find it? It's all your fault!"

She stomps away in a huff, and a terrible realization slams me between the eyes. Those aren't the only pictures on Jess's cell phone. There's also the series I took of her dancing with Jason, including the one with him holding his nose in the "Rock Lobster" fish dance. If Brooke sends *those* pictures around — and I'm certain she will — Jess will know I was lying when I told her I didn't use her phone.

And she'd never forgive me. She already thinks this whole disaster is my fault — and really, she's right. The thought of Jess getting so mad that she might end our friendship is simply too awful to face.

I have to do something to fix this. But how?

Chapter Five

I get off the bus at my usual stop and walk to the cleaners. I'm ten minutes early, and if I wasn't feeling so utterly sick over Jess, I'd probably go to Sam's Diner and order something from the Fats, Oils, and Sweets group. But all I can think of is how I can get my best friend's phone back before Brooke sends out any more photos.

I have the number, of course: Jess's cell phone is first on my contact list. I could call Brooke right now and . . . and what? Say, "Stop doing this, please?" Offer her some kind of bribe? What could I possibly offer a girl who wears real gold jewelry to a school dance?

I think about asking my dad for advice, but he's out

making sales calls. This means MacInerny's in charge. If there's anything worse than her usual self, it's her usual self on a power trip.

Cat has first shift at the customer counter again, and as soon as I've put on my name tag and smock, I start rolling cartloads of newly tagged clothes to the back to be sorted and cleaned.

Cat and I like to dish about incoming garments, and there are some excellent candidates in today's mix, including a fuzzy orange coat that looks like a cat's scratching post. But with MacInerny hovering over our every move, we have to make do with flashing each other thumbs up, down, or sideways behind her back.

At one point, though, there's a lull between customers, and our supervisor goes over to Sam's to pick up a snack. "Think she'll splurge on the chicken rice soup or the onion broth?" Cat asks.

"Cream of wheat," I say. "Anything hideous in the cart?"

"Something for Nelson," says Cat. "Check these out." She picks up a pair of kelly green golf pants, split all the way down the rear seam.

"Think he got a hole in one?" I laugh.

So does Cat. "And look at *this* tasteful ensemble!" She reaches deep into the cart for a lavender church-lady pant-suit with grass-stained knees. "Perfect for every occasion, from pet cemetery to badminton court. That needs stain removal, so put it on Rose's pile."

Stain removal. The phrase jogs my memory, and my pulse races. Elise. All of a sudden I remember Elise on the day Jess came in. In the changing room, holding her cousin's school uniform. Navy blue blazer, plaid skirt . . .

I catch my breath. Could it be?

"Right back," I say, bombing through the doors into the workroom before Cat has a chance to ask why.

I make a beeline for Special Care. The stain specialist, Rose, has been home sick since Thursday, so there's quite a pile at her station. I paw through it greedily, holding my breath. Sure enough, right on the bottom, I spot a plaid skirt and a navy blue jacket. I pick up the blazer. There's a gold crest over the left pocket, and my eyes go big with disbelief.

Score! It's a Foreman Academy blazer!

This is it. This is the answer!

A plan is already starting to form in my brain as I grab the plaid skirt. Like the blazer, it's spattered with paint, but that doesn't matter, as long as it helps me get past the security guard and onto the campus.

I know it's crazy, but I simply have to do this. My friendship with Jess is at stake.

I head for the locker room to stash the uniform in my locker, when I hear Elise's voice.

"Where are you going with Annika's uniform?"

I wince. As sweet and fun as she is, Elise is a total rule follower. She didn't approve of me and Cat sneaking off to a Broadway premiere . . . but when push came to shove, she helped me out anyway. I turn toward her and blurt out, "I need it."

She arches an eyebrow. "You *need* it?"

I confess the whole cell phone story. "So if I could borrow that uniform, just to get into the school —"

"Whoa, hold on, Diana. That's already been tagged. It's in the computer. It's coded for special care. You can't just take home customers' clothes."

"I'm not taking it home. I just need it to get past the gatehouse and rescue Jess's phone. Could you possibly give me a ride after work?"

"I've got basketball practice. Anyway, I wouldn't —"

"Fine," I say hastily. "But could you at least pretend you didn't see this?"

Elise looks at me for a long moment. "See what?" she finally says, and I feel like hugging her.

Next I try Cat, who gives me the eye. "Diana, you gotta stop sneaking around like this."

"You don't understand. This is totally, utterly urgent. My best friend is furious at me." My voice sounds so desperate that she relents.

"All right, fine, but it can't be today. I don't even have Jared's van — he's picking me up after work."

"But it's urgent! Would *he* drive?"

"Diana, my boyfriend is *not* gonna go for this insane scam of yours. How about tomorrow? We get out of school at eleven for some staff-development thing, and I'm free till I start here at three."

"We've got a half day, too. Must be the whole district. That's perfect!" I'm clutching the blue blazer like it's

82

going to save my life. Which, who knows, it actually might.

"Pssst. Mac Attack." Cat picks up her stapler, restapling a numbered tag into the lavender pantsuit as Miss MacInerny comes in with a hot cup of something that smells like old broccoli. "So. Special Care for that and the lavender one with the grass stains, okay?" Cat says loudly to me.

"Got it," I reply gratefully, rolling the cart through the double doors. Once I'm in the back, it's no problem to smuggle the uniform into the locker room. On my way out, I make a quick detour to the No Pickup rack to look for a plain white blouse, but I don't spot one. Too bad. That would have been perfect.

As I push my cart back toward the customer counter, Elise calls out from the bagging machine, "I could use a hand here if you're free."

"I'll be there in a minute. I have to take something to Nelson."

I carry the split green pants up to the Tailoring section. Nelson stands at the cutting table, carefully pinning hand-cut pattern pieces onto a sequined white jumpsuit.

83

I stare at it. "What in the world — ?"

Nelson barely looks at me. "Elvis impersonator in Atlantic City. Took over the gig from a guy who was six inches taller and ate more like Elvis did."

"Speaking of which . . ." I hold up the split pants.

Nelson sighs, shaking his head as he takes them out of my hands. "They don't pay me enough for this."

My heart stops a little. He better not try asking Dad for a raise when his job is already in jeopardy. I hesitate. Should I say something? I'd like to give Nelson fair warning — if it was me, I'd want to know sooner than later — but I hate to spread rumors. Besides, I'm not supposed to know anything about this, and I wouldn't want Dad to find out I was eavesdropping.

I must have a strange look on my face, because Nelson says, "What?" in an impatient tone.

"Nothing," I tell him, and roll out my best imitation of *Project Runway*'s Tim Gunn. "Make it work."

Nelson retaliates with a German-accented "Sorry, Diana, you're *out*."

How could Dad even think about firing him?

• • •

Elise and Cat take turns running the bagging machine, which I'm not supposed to use. But I help them assemble each order, twist-tying hangers together and putting them on the conveyor belt in numerical order. This last part is more fun than it sounds, since the conveyor is operated by a foot pedal. I love standing there watching hundreds of garments swish past till I find the right number. I used to call it the Dress Parade when I was little.

Today I'm on a mission. As the Dress Parade swishes before my eyes, I'm looking for two things at once: the right place to hang up each order, and a white blouse, my size. I have to be subtle about it — Elise would definitely object to me borrowing something that's already cleaned. But I got the idea from Nelson, who likes to go out after hours in designer clothes and bring them back in for recleaning. It's our little secret. I lift my foot off the pedal to slow it down so many times that Elise starts to wonder about it.

"Foot cramp," I tell her.

"Want me to take over?"

"I'm fine," I say hastily, spotting a white blouse as it travels past on the conveyor. I make mental note of its number for later.

85

Finally it's time for my afternoon break. Elise goes up front to fill in at the customer counter, and Cat and I take our ten minutes together. The first thing I do is circle the Dress Parade, pulling down four clean white blouses.

Mr. Chen looks up from his steam presser as we carry the bagged items past him, so I cover by saying to Cat, "I'm sure the fifth one's on the No Pickup rack. We'll just check the tag numbers till we get a match."

"Good one," she says when we get out of earshot.

"Acting improvisation," I say. "Helps you think on your feet."

"I could use some of that, dating Jared!" She laughs as I open the door to the fur storage vault.

This is the most private place in Cinderella Cleaners, and no one will bat an eye at us going inside, since it's also the coolest and quietest. Sometimes we take our afternoon breaks in there just to hang out in the air-conditioning. Okay, and secretly try on a mink coat or two.

But today it's not coats that I want to try on. I leave Cat to check the blouse sizes, and hurry back to the locker room to fetch the blue blazer and skirt.

"These two look the best," says Cat when I return. "I

went to Catholic school till I was ten. I've done time in a uniform."

The blouse is no problem — the first one I try is exactly my size — but the plaid skirt's too big in the waist. "Safety pin," Cat says. "No problem."

Now for the blazer. This is the worst fit yet — too tight in the shoulders and short in the sleeves — but I'm stuck with it.

"How do I look?" I ask, without much hope.

"Like you're wearing your kid sister's uniform." Cat points at the paint stain. "Right after her finger-paint class."

"Can it pass in a pinch?"

Cat hesitates, and I know in my heart that the answer is no. "It would help a whole lot if you let out the cuffs," she says finally.

I roll back a sleeve. There are a few inches of extra fabric. "Letting them out is no problem. It's putting them *back*. There's a lining."

Cat shrugs. "Beg Nelson to help you. You know he will. We better get back to work, or Mac Attack's gonna come after us."

No sooner has she said the word than the door to the storage vault opens. Both of us gasp, and I jump behind Cat's back. But it's only Elise, with a pink order slip in her hand.

"Some guy wants to pick up his shearling," she says. Then she looks at me. "Let me see that."

Sheepishly, I step out from behind Cat, expecting a lecture about trying on clothes during work hours. But Elise bursts out laughing.

"You look just like Annika!"

"Really?" This could be unbelievably useful.

"Well, she's a bit shorter, with frizzier hair. And she wears glasses."

Good to know. "Tell me about her."

Elise shrugs. "She's fourteen years old and a total klutz. She's always got paint on her clothing. She practically lives in that giant arts building they've got over there."

Annika sounds like my kind of woman.

"What's her last name?" I ask.

Elise narrows her eyes at me. "Why?"

"Just curious."

She shakes her head. "You better not try any —"

"Annika Reed," says Cat quickly.

Elise looks at her, startled. "How did you know that?"

Grinning, Cat holds up the customer tag she's unpinned. "This is a dry cleaner, *chica*. Nobody's got any secrets from us."

I go home feeling better about my disguise. Nelson has lent me a stitch ripper to take out the hems of the blazer sleeves. "Be sure you iron them well, or your wrists will have stripes," he warns me. He even agrees to redo the hems in the same kind of stitch when I bring the blazer back to the cleaners. Nelson is the bomb.

As soon as I've finished the dishes from dinner, I go up to my room to iron the sleeves and try out different hairstyles. Parting my hair way too far to one side does two things at once: It makes me look different, and covers up part of my face. If I sleep with it wet and in braids, it'll also be frizzier when I unbraid it. For once, I'm happy my hair is plain brown and not Jess's show-stopping red. When you have dark hair and eyes and you're medium tall, it's easy to look a little like a lot of other people.

I sort through my jewelry, looking for something as different as possible from the dangly Indian earrings I wore to the dance. Probably no one would notice but me, but when you're getting into a character, detail is everything.

After several tries, I go with plain pearls. That should look kind of preppy. I hope. Remembering Brooke's pale pink manicure, I do my nails. They're short, and the only polish I have is flamingo pink, but I paint it on anyway.

Next I dig out an old pair of black Mary Janes that are bound to pass better than Converse with two different laces. The final touch is a pair of thick tortoiseshell glasses I wore in a school play two years ago.

I check out my look in the mirror. I'm not completely transformed, but if I slump my shoulders and cross my arms over my chest in a don't-look-at-me posture, I'm not going to stand out in a crowd. Especially when everyone else in the crowd is wearing the same clothes.

I'm practicing looking like somebody else when my phone rings. *Must be Jess with her usual check-in*, I think, feeling glad she's using her landline instead of just sulking about her stolen phone.

But it isn't Jess — or rather, it *is* Jess's phone. Brooke's used it to send out an even worse photograph.

This one shows Jess in the Foreman Academy bathroom, caught with her eyes bulging and mouth wide open. It must be the one she snapped just as she saw the door opening. But it's the text message that stops my heart:

who do i luv? more 2 come ;)

That can only mean one thing. The next shot Brooke sends will be one of the ones I took of Jess dancing with Jason. And I'm positive I know which one: the "Rock Lobster" shot where he's holding his nose and she looks like a fish.

Aaahh!!

Chapter Six

Half days at school are a total waste. Every period winds up so short that the teachers don't want to get anything started, so most of them give us study hall time or show movies. They might as well just let us sleep late.

Jess is in the worst mood on the planet today, and she's barely speaking to me. Not only is everyone asking her questions and joking about that last photo, but she has to go straight home after school and make lunch for Dash, since their mom is working till four and it's too long to leave him without supervision.

"As if I could supervise *him*," she tells Sara bitterly. "*Supervision* is just a big word for we'll fight with each other till Mom gets off her shift. I wish you could come over."

"Sorry," says Sara, shooting a sidelong glance at me. "My mother wants me to come home."

I've already told everyone I have stuff to do at the cleaners, and that Cat is picking me up after school. Sure enough, when we get out to the curb, Jared's van is pulled up at the end of the long line of school buses.

I hop into the passenger seat next to Cat. "Hey, those braids are cute," she says as I buckle my seat belt.

"I'm hoping they'll turn my hair frizzy."

She starts up the van. "You got all your stuff?"

I'm already wearing the earrings and shoes, and I've stashed the rolled blazer and skirt in my backpack, along with the glasses and a map of the campus I printed last night. Yesterday, Cat hid the blouse, still in its cleaner bag, under a tarp in the back of the van. All I need now is a place I can change.

"Don't sweat it," says Cat. "This is a drivable dressing room. I'll pull over at one of those lookout points up on the cliffs." She turns on the radio, singing along like she always does.

Sure enough, a few miles out of town we come to a parking lot next to a heavy stone wall and a couple of coin-operated viewing machines that look like they've been there for ages. It's one of those clear but crisp days, when it's warm in the sunshine and cold in the shade, and the wind has the snap of a freshly picked apple.

I climb into the back of the van, which is full of guy stuff like free weights and a DayGlo orange Frisbee. I've met Jared a couple of times, and he seems nice enough, but so different from Cat that it's hard to imagine them being a couple. He's on his school's wrestling team, and his whole life is sports.

I crouch down and peel off the sweater I'm wearing over my cami, swapping it for the white blouse. Then I pull on the plaid skirt, safety-pin its loose waistband, and wiggle out of my funky striped leggings. I unroll the blazer and pull it on, tugging the sleeves down as far as I can. I'm starting to get butterflies in my stomach, as if I'm backstage in the dressing room.

"How's it going back there?" Cat calls over the radio.

"Good." I make my way back to the front seat and fasten my seat belt. As Cat pulls away from the parking lot, I unbraid my hair. Just as I hoped, it's wavy and full. With the side part, it covers a lot of my face.

When we reach the next stoplight, I put on the tortoise-shell glasses and turn toward Cat. "What do you think?"

She glances my way. "You're a total Before picture."

"That was the plan. I'm going for stealth moves."

"Is that what you call it?"

We're driving along the cast-iron fence that surrounds the Foreman Academy. I'm reviewing my plan in my head. Get into the girls' dorm, figure out which room is Brooke's, find the phone. Of course, there's a chance it won't *be* in her room, that she's got it with her, in which case I'll have to step up to Plan B. But I'm hoping I won't have to face her.

"The gatehouse is right up ahead, but you better drive past it to let me out. I don't want the security guard to see me getting out of the van."

Cat nods and drives past the gatehouse, slowing slightly to look down the driveway. She lets out a low whistle. "Whoa. This is some crib."

"I know, right?"

There's an ice cream stand just down the road. Cat pulls in and parks. "I bet all the preppies come in here to get milkshakes and stuff," she says as I open the door and climb out. "Unless they all drink light Frappuccinos. What time do you want me to pick you up?"

"Quarter of three, I guess. Right before work."

She frowns. "It's not even noon yet."

"I'm not sure how long it'll take. But if I get out sooner, I'll wait inside. I'll be the one drinking a milkshake."

"Okay," she says. "Be careful. I don't want to be posting your bail for impersonating a rich girl."

"I promise." Cat gives me a high five through the open window and drives away. I'm all by myself. I can feel my heart pounding, but can't really tell if I'm scared or excited. The ice cream stand has a big window, and I can see my reflection. I look pretty different from the girl who went to the Foreman dance Saturday night, but the question is, can I pass for Annika Reed? And there's only one way to find out.

I walk back along the fence until I reach the gatehouse. Leaning forward so my frizzy hair covers more of my face, I nod toward the guard at the window and walk quickly past.

"Hold on there," he says. "I need your pass."

Pass? Oh, no! I didn't think of *that*. I dig around in the blazer's right pocket, and then in the left. "I must have dropped it," I stammer.

"What time did you sign out?" The guard is a fatherly African-American man wearing thick glasses that are a lot like the ones I have on. I hope this will cause him to like me.

"Um, early?" *Before you came on duty, whenever that was.*

"Was Nick still on shift?" *Sure, whatever you say.*

"Nick, right," I nod, hoping that he'll let me pass, but he takes out a clipboard with signatures.

"What's your name?"

"Annika Reed," I say, wincing and crossing my fingers that he doesn't know Elise's cousin by sight.

"Reed?" he says, scanning the list with a frown.

I'm cooked. I won't even get onto the campus before I get kicked out. I stare at his clipboard list, trying to read upside down. "There was a UPS truck coming in at the same time. About nine in the morning?" I *hope* that's a nine I see next to his hand.

"Here it is — 9:05 A.M." He points. "Nick wrote down the truck coming in, but not you going out."

"Well, he gave me a pass," I say, trying to sound just impatient enough to move this along. "Is there some kind of problem? Just sign me back in."

I guess attitude does the trick, because he looks at me, sighs, and writes down ANNA K. REED and the time. "You hold on to your pass next time, hear?" I nod and he waves me through.

Now what?

My heart pounds extra loud as I walk down the long driveway onto the campus. It's even more beautiful here in the sunlight. There's no one in sight but a few men in gardeners' uniforms, riding lawn mowers and using leaf blowers. The buildings look different — brighter and less Gothic-spooky than they did at night. But I can remember the layout from Jason's tour, and I've studied the map from the Web site.

There's the gym, right next to Parking Lot B. The boys' and girls' dorms are behind it, across from the quad with the main classroom building and clock tower. The cafeteria — oops, *dining hall* — is that low, glass-front building next to the library, and right behind that, I can make out the white marble top of the Abercrombie Arts Center.

Got it, I think, feeling proud of myself. *Next stop, girls' dorm.*

I wonder what these students' bedrooms are like. Do they each have a room to themselves, or are there great big dorm rooms with bunk beds in rows, like the YMCA camp in the Poconos where we took our seventh-grade field trip? What time is their curfew, if they even have one?

I think about how fun it would be, sharing a dorm room with Jess and Amelia and Sara. It sounds like a year-long pajama party. No parents to make you do homework. No *Fay*. Wow. I'm liking the sound of this better and better, and my steps speed up as I head toward the dorm. I can't wait to see what it looks like.

The clock tower says it's a little past noon, which seems like it ought to be lunchtime, but the only students I see are playing lacrosse on a manicured field in the distance, behind the gym. Maybe the Foreman Academy school day starts later than ours, which begins at the unholy hour of seven thirty A.M. If so, they might still be in their morning classes. Good. Then the dorm should be empty.

I hope there are names on the doors. Then I wonder what Brooke's last name is, and whether there's more than one Brooke at the Foreman Academy. Why didn't I think of this before? And what if she keeps her room locked? I'll be out of luck. The mission I've set for myself seems completely impossible. But I can't let Brooke send out those photos! It may be a long shot, but it's all I've got.

A stern-looking teacher comes out of the main classroom building. When he gets down the stairs and turns onto the path, he'll be heading right toward me. I double back, dodging behind a tall hedge, where I nearly bump into a large bearded man holding clippers.

"Sorry!" I squeak. "Late for gym."

"You sure are," he says, sounding amused.

I scuttle along the inside of the hedge as far as I can and dart into the gym building. It seems weirdly quiet, but maybe the students are all outside on the lacrosse field. I remember that the side door behind the bandstand faced onto the dorms, so I tiptoe down the long oak-paneled hall, under the eyes of the headmaster portraits. They look so real that I almost expect one of them to ask me for a password and open the door to the Gryffindor common room.

The gym looks completely deserted, so I start across its wide polished floor. All of a sudden, there's a clatter of footsteps and voices from the equipment room. I duck under the bleachers and flatten myself to the wall as the students come in. I'm astonished to see they're all dressed in white uniforms, carrying mesh masks and *swords*.

It's a fencing class!

I feel a rush of excitement.

I've watched *Pirates of the Caribbean* and *The Princess Bride* about a hundred and fifty times each, and *The Parent Trap* with twin Lindsay Lohans fighting a duel with each other. I'm a total sucker for sword-fighting scenes. I'd give anything to be able to do that.

There is nothing even half this cool in Weehawken Middle School gym classes. We either play lame imitations of actual sports, like crab soccer, flag football, and floor hockey, or else we just do calisthenics. If the gym teacher's feeling inspired, we might go outside and jog around the track. Unless you're a jock like Amelia, it's totally boring.

The thought of a school where you get to take fencing and outdoor lacrosse, not to mention theatre and filmmaking, gives me a real pang of envy. I almost forget to be scared I'll get caught.

Well, almost.

The coach is a no-nonsense woman with sandy brown hair, wearing blue and gold Foreman Academy sweats. She blows a whistle, and everyone lines up along a white stripe on one side of the gym.

"Salute!" she says, and everyone raises and lowers their swords in unison.

"En garde!" The fencers put the masks over their heads and assume a ready position, half crouched, with one leg facing forward and one to the side. They look so professional!

"Ready?" They raise their swords.

"And go. Attack, attack, attack. Retreat, retreat, retreat."

On every "attack" the whole line steps forward; on every "retreat," they all step back. Holding my breath, I keep hoping they won't retreat *too* much. It's dark down here under the bleachers, but I'm not invisible. Even to people in wire-mesh masks.

The coach drills them forward and backward, some-times adding a "Lunge!" which makes them all giant-step forward with one foot and thrust out their swords as if they're stabbing enemies. It looks totally fun, and I wish I could stay in the shadows and watch the whole class — or better yet, put on a mask and try fencing myself. But some-one might spot me, and anyway, I have to get to the dorm before classes let out.

I work my way down to the end of the bleachers and wait for my moment. As soon as the line travels all the way forward, so everyone's facing away from the bleachers, I scuttle across to the door, push it open, and rush outside. I hope hope hope that no one heard me.

Whew! Now I'm out in the sunshine, facing the dorms. Girls on the left and boys on the right. Or is it the other way around? I pull the map out of my pocket to double-check.

Maybe that's why I don't hear the gym door open.

"Hey!" says a voice right behind me. I whip around, frantic. One of the fencers, a girl, is striding toward me, gesturing at the paint on my sleeve and skirt. "How come you're wearing my uniform?"

Oh . . . no.

My stomach drops.

Here's something *else* I hadn't counted on.

I stare at the white-covered figure. "Annika . . . Annika Reed?"

Annika takes off her fencing mask, shaking out a wild mop of dark hair as she studies my face. Her glasses look like Tina Fey's. "Do I know you?" she asks, frowning at me.

"I'm a friend of your cousin," I stammer.

"Which one?" she demands.

"Elise," I say, praying that Annika won't turn me in to security. "We work at the cleaners together. Cinderella Cleaners. "

Annika stares for a few seconds more. Then, to my shock, she grins. "Cool beans! So what's up? Are you supposed to be *me*?"

I'm so relieved I nearly fall over. "Sort of."

"Then lose the pearl earrings. I wouldn't wear those to a funeral," she says. I notice she's got several holes in each ear, though they're empty right now; probably gym class rules. "May I ask *why* you're pretending you're me?"

I'm not really sure where to start. I'm just so happy that Annika doesn't seem evil. But before I can speak, the same stern-looking teacher I spotted before comes around the corner. Is he following me?

"Where are you two supposed to be?" he demands.

Annika holds up her mask. "Fencing?" she says in a tone that stops just short of mocking. Like, why else would I have a face mask and sword, *hello*?

"I suggest you get back there," he snaps. He's a tall, bony man with a tuft of hair on each side of his bald spot.

"Sure, Mr. Wilcox. Whatever you say." Annika heads for the door. I'm sorry to see her go — it seemed like she might really help. But I turn and start to walk in the other direction.

"Where do you think you're going?" says Mr. Wilcox. I freeze.

"Um . . . to my dorm room?" I stutter.

"During class?" Mr. Wilcox stares down his long nose. "Where are you supposed to be now?" Wordless with fear, I point to one side of the main classroom building, where Jason said there's a big science lecture hall. "Go back there immediately. You can go to your dorm after lunch."

I don't dare argue with him. I'm just thankful he didn't ask for my name. I turn and walk toward the lecture hall with my heart sinking into my shoes. How is *this* going to work?

But Mr. Wilcox isn't done with me yet. I can feel his eyes on my back as he barks out his parting shot. "And get that uniform cleaned!"

Chapter Seven

The lecture hall is big and dark with seats in steep banks on three sides of the room. When I open the door in back, it lets in bright light from the hall, and a few faces turn to see who's come in. I dip my head, quickly closing the door behind me as I enter.

Are Brooke and her friend in this class? What grade is this, anyway? I'm completely confused, but I have no choice but to take a seat.

The teacher stands down in the center, showing a Power Point presentation that seems to involve an erupting volcano, with loud sound effects and fiery flashes. He's a silver-haired man with a square but jowly face and a deep voice that sounds like the actors who narrate the previews for movies. The blue glow coming up from his laptop screen makes him look even more melodramatic.

"When the magma reaches the earth's surface, it is called *lava*. It may erupt violently, sending *pyroclastic rocks* tumbling, and spewing ash and dust particles into the air," he says in a rolling voice that would put me to sleep in minutes. So maybe not every class in prep school is exciting or cool.

Just as I slide into one of the few empty seats at the back of the room, the teacher snaps the lights back on. Students squint and groan and shift around, and I feel totally exposed.

What if he saw me sneak in?

"Right, then," the teacher says briskly. "Who can tell me the three kinds of lava? Trevor?" A broad-shouldered boy in the front row makes some weird sounds, ending with "pillow."

"Correct. *A'a*, *pahoehoe*, and *pillow lava*." Voice-Over Man types all three names onto the Smart Board projector. "And what are their characteristics? Somebody else."

He scans the back rows, and I squinch deeper into my seat, hoping he won't call on *me* for an answer. His eyes fall on me for a second, and I'm insanely relieved when the bell on the clock tower chimes.

"Ladies and gentlemen, class is *dismissed*," the teacher intones with a little half bow, as if he's expecting a curtain call.

All around me, students stand up, gather notebooks and backpacks, and stream toward the doors. Adjusting my hair and glasses for maximum coverage, I join the crowd, hoping there's safety in numbers.

But when we get outside the lecture hall, nobody heads for the dorms. It's like a lava flow of blue uniforms, heading straight for the doors of the dining hall. I better follow the herd. I keep an eye out for tall blondes, but Brooke and her sidekick don't seem to be taking earth science, or Hawaiian studies, or whatever this class was. *That's a relief,* I think as I join the crowd streaming into the dining hall. The faculty monitor standing next to the door doesn't pay any attention to me — I'm just one more hungry kid in a navy blue blazer.

Inside, it's a different story. Unlike the science lecture hall, the dining hall's flooded with sunlight, and students are sitting at round tables, facing each other in small groups of friends. There's no way I'm *not* going to be noticed by somebody as an outsider. Should I walk back out? Would the door monitor question me this time around? Or should I forget the girls' dorm and switch to Plan B: Look for Brooke and try a direct approach? Maybe if I ask her point-blank, she'll just give me Jess's phone.

Sure she will.

I'm not sure what to do, but I am really hungry. It's been a long time since my morning o.j. and bagel, and the dining hall food smells . . . delicious. Might as well get some lunch while I plot my next move.

This place makes the Weehawken Middle School cafeteria look like a soup kitchen. There's a hot buffet serving everything from Thai food to homemade ravioli, with real china plates and silverware instead of Styrofoam and plastic sporks. There's an actual sushi station, and the salad bar looks like the one at the fancy steakhouse where we held grandpapa's retirement party, with juicy tomatoes and fresh avocados and three types of lettuce. There's even a whole row of different dressings, plus croutons and bacon bits, crumbles of feta cheese, and sunflower seeds. A girl could get used to this.

I pile my plate high and look around for a safe place to sit, choosing one of the few empty tables. I can't wait to dig into that yummy salad. Keeping my head low, I skulk toward the back of the room. But before I've gone more than five steps, Brooke appears out of nowhere. With her sidekick. I've got one blonde on each side of me. No place to hide.

Where did they come from?

"New girl, huh?" says Brooke.

"*Nice* blazer," her friend smirks, eyeballing the paint stains.

I'm busted!

I better jump straight to Plan B. But just as I'm about to start blurting about Jess's phone, Brooke says, "Just what we need around here. More art geeks."

Suddenly I realize something amazing: Brooke and her sidekick don't have a clue who I am. Their mean is *generic* mean — picking on somebody new with bad hair and glasses and paint on her uniform — not *specific* mean: picking on *me*. My disguise must have worked! Either that, or they were so focused on redheaded Jess at the dance that her brunette friend faded into the woodwork.

Whatever. The point is, I haven't been recognized . . . yet.

Thinking fast, I act like somebody who always gets picked on, a meek, cringing newbie frightened by popular girls. It isn't that hard to snap right into character: I just have to channel the way I felt when Kayleigh came to Cinderella Cleaners and saw me in my smock.

"I spilled paint in my art class," I whisper, ducking my eyes toward the floor. I turn my toes inward and hunch my shoulders, trying to disappear.

"Too bad," says Brooke, oozing fake sympathy. "Art is so *messy*. It ruins your nails. Right, Mackenzie?"

"The worst," smirks her sidekick Mackenzie, staring at my short, badly polished nails gripping my tray. "Hey, what's your name? Maybe we'll give you a newcomer makeover."

"Make yourselves over and leave her alone," says a boy's voice behind me. I twist around quickly and face a curly-haired boy in a Foreman blazer.

It's Jason!

Brooke looks completely shocked. Her hand flies up to

her hair in a caught-in-the-act gesture. If she weren't so mean, I'd feel sorry for her — picking on strangers is *not* how you want to be seen by a boy you like.

"Jason!" she says in a totally different voice, coated with sugar. "I didn't see you come in."

"Lucky me," Jason says, and it's all I can do not to laugh out loud. Burn!

Mackenzie gasps, sputtering. *Nobody* treats the queen bee like that. "*Hey!*" she says angrily.

"Hay is for horses," says Jason, and this time I *do* laugh. "Come on," he says, grabbing my elbow and steering me quickly away.

"How did you —" I whisper.

"Just keep walking," he says to me under his breath as we pass through the crowd. "I'll get you out of here."

"But that monitor watching the door —"

"I know him, Diana. Just leave it to me." Jason looks down at my sleeve, where the paint stain is, and swerves me toward the condiment bar.

"What are you doing?"

"That's ketchup. Get mad at me. Really mad."

All of a sudden I get it. I nod and carry my salad to the condiment bar, where Jason "accidentally" bumps into me. Our timing is perfect, as if we've rehearsed it.

"*Hey!*" I echo Mackenzie. "You just, like, *totally* ruined my blazer!" I plunk my tray down on the table.

"My bad," Jason says as heads swivel our way. I look down at my splattered sleeve, hiding my face as he rushes me past the door monitor.

"I'm *so* embarrassed!" I wail.

"They've got stain remover at Housekeeping. Back in a few, Mr. Cook."

The door monitor steps aside for us, nodding sympathetically, and Jason and I are outside.

"That was awesome!" I say as we hurry away from the building.

"Classic! You sounded like someone who actually goes here. 'You, like, totally *ruined* my blazer, you peasant.' You've got it down." Jason grins at me.

"Thanks." I grin back, and his face gets more serious.

"Can I ask you a question?"

I know what it is. "As in, what am I doing here?"

"That, too, but . . . why is Jess mad at me? I've called

her three times and she never picks up. She keeps sending these really mean texts."

I gulp. I didn't think of this, but Brooke must have heard every one of his messages — and put him onto the phone's contact list.

"It's not Jess," I tell Jason emphatically.

"It's not?" He sounds very relieved.

"Brooke stole Jess's phone at the dance. She's been sending those texts to Jess's whole contact list. Everyone but her mom."

Jason shakes his head. "That is so Foreman. Leave it to Brookenzie."

"Brookenzie?" I laugh again. That's perfect! They really are two of a kind.

Jason looks at my Foreman Academy uniform. "I guess this would explain why you're wearing that getup?"

"I thought I'd be unrecognizable."

"The glasses are good, and the hair, but no. Not in the face. I knew who you were right away."

I sigh, depressed that my disguise isn't as fool-proof as I thought. "Brooke and Mackenzie didn't," I point out.

"That's because all they notice is clothes. So how can I help you?"

"I need to get into Brooke's dorm room."

Jason stops in his tracks and lets out a low whistle. "Oh, man. Inner sanctum. If there's one rule the Foreman Academy really enforces, it's 'No boys in the girls' dorm.' Ever. Grounds for expulsion."

"Wow. Serious."

"Not that I'd mind getting kicked out of here, but my parents might have a few issues with it."

I finally get the chance to ask what I've been wondering about since the dance. "Why don't you like this place? I think it's great!"

Jason shrugs, surveying the campus, from the perfect lawns to the new arts complex. "It *looks* pretty nice from the outside, I guess . . . but it's the people." He looks me right in the eye. "They're all so competitive. It's all about getting a 4.0 grade average and where you'll be going to law school, and what color Porsche you'll be driving to your second home. Everybody at Foreman is walking around with a chip on their shoulder, like they think they should get a free pass because their family's rich. And everyone knows whose father owns what, whose mother is famous. Nobody sees you for you."

I never thought of that side of it. "That sounds really messed up."

Jason smiles ruefully, flashing those Nick Jonas dimples Jess fell for. "I could use a few friends in the real world, I guess."

I see what he means. Jess and Sara and Amelia and I might not be privileged preppies, but no one would ever say my friends aren't real. And I'm suddenly grateful for that. "Well, you just made two new ones," I say. "Me and Jess."

Jason's smile widens. "Sweet. So let's go get her phone."

Chapter Eight

We're outside the girls' dorm. "This is as far as I go," Jason says, stopping next to a flower bed. "They have Y chromosome sensors hidden in every tree."

I squint up at the three-story building. It looks like a fortress. "Any idea which room might be Brooke's?"

The idea seems hopeless, but Jason surprises me. "Actually, yes. In English last week, she was gushing about her new pink-and-green curtains. I thought she was going to write a whole essay about them."

I scan the ground floor from left to right. Not a pink or green curtain in sight. None on the second floor either. I'm about to lose hope when Jason says, "Bingo!"

I look where he's pointing. The very last window on the third floor sports a pair of ruffled plaid curtains in lime green and hot pink. They manage to look both expensive and tacky, like somebody's Lilly Pulitzer dress morphed into an awning.

"Of course she'd be on the top floor," Jason says.

Yes, of course. Hardest room in the building to get in and out of. I take a deep breath.

"Any tips on breaking and entering?" I ask, already feeling like a criminal. What if they dust for fingerprints?

"Nothing too helpful. You'll have to get past the R.A."

"What's that?"

"Residential advisor. She's kind of the den mother for the girls' dorm. Sits at the front desk to repel Foreman boys."

My stomach sinks. "So she'll know every girl in the building."

"Basically, yeah." We look at each other. The odds seem impossible, but I can't give up now.

"I could create a distraction," says Jason. "It works in the movies."

"What kind of distraction?"

He looks around, clearly trying to spot something useful. I notice three girls coming toward us. They're wearing the same navy blazers and plaid skirts as everyone else, but with a twist. One girl, who looks biracial, wears her blond-ish hair in a fountain of dreadlocks. The second girl has spiky black hair and green Doc Marten boots. And the third girl has Tina Fey glasses and frizzy dark hair.

I do a double-take at the third girl. It's Annika Reed!

She's wearing a patterned silk headband, mix-and-match earrings, and seven or eight bangle bracelets on each of her wrists. It's as if she's determined to make every inch that's not covered by Foreman Academy uniform fabric completely her own. If we went to the same school, I bet we'd be friends. And if I know the codes of middle school clothes, her arty headband, arms full of bracelets, and checkered Vans send the message that she's a rebel outsider who can't stand the popular crowd. She'll probably be on my side.

"Annika!" I call out, waving as if we're old friends.

She looks puzzled, then gets it. "Look, it's the other me," I hear her tell her friends as they approach.

It's funny how even a uniform can't tamp down people's style. I'd hate to be stuck in the same outfit every day, and

I'm sure I'd find small ways to personalize my look, just as these three do.

Annika stops before me, putting her hands on her hips and smiling. "So, Other Me, have you got a name?"

"Diana," I tell her.

"Cool. This is Nico and Lexy." She nods at her friends. "Can you finally tell me why you're wearing my uniform?"

"Long story. Short version: I need to get into the dorm." The three of them look at me, waiting for more, and I suddenly get an idea. "Will you help walk me past the R.A.?"

Annika glances over at Jason. "Diana's cool," he says. "She's got my stamp of approval."

"*Your* stamp? Oh, well, that's all that matters." She's being sarcastic, but I get the feeling she doesn't mind him. It's how Jess would kid with Ethan or Will. There's this tone that girls take with a boy who's a friend to make sure no one thinks he's a *boyfriend*.

"Please?" I say, hoping I don't sound too desperate.

Annika shrugs. "Sure, why not. I can't stand this place anyway. Too many rules."

"You got that right," says Nico, the girl with blond dreads. Lexy, the spike-haired girl, nods in agreement. I know kids complain about school even when they don't actually hate it, but so far, it's four big thumbs-down on the Foreman Academy. Is it really that bad, or are preppy kids just more demanding? But I don't have time to think about this. I need to get into Brooke's dorm room before she comes back from lunch.

Jason wishes me luck, and the four of us start toward the dorm. "Where are you going once you get inside?" Annika asks me.

"Third floor. Where's the staircase?"

"End of the hall," says Nico.

"Our room's on the third floor," says Lexy. "Just follow us."

"Which side is the desk?" I ask Annika, and she looks at me blankly. "The R.A. desk."

"Oh. On the left." I step to the right, and the other three girls swarm around me in a protective wedge.

"Girl pack," says Annika. "We've got you covered."

I nod, but my heart's beating fast as we head through the door. When we pass the R.A.'s desk, Annika takes the lead in a loud conversation about a boy in their studio art class. "Could you believe that's what he calls a life drawing? I've seen coatracks with more sense of motion."

The other girls laugh, and I pitch in a "Really." Better not use my voice more than I have to.

"And how about that proportion? His head was the size of an *orange*." She's a good improviser. The residential advisor barely looks up at the cluster of uniformed art students chatting as we head for the stairs. That's one hurdle passed.

Once we get on the stairs, out of earshot, Annika turns to me. "It's Diana, right?"

"Right."

"Whose room did you say you were looking for?"

"I didn't, but Brooke's."

Annika stops in her tracks. So do the other two. "Brooke Fontaine? Is your *friend*?"

"No way. She stole my friend's cell phone. I'm taking it back."

Annika's eyes go wide. "You can't mess with Brooke Fontaine!" she says. "Her family owns Newport, Rhode Island. She'll have you deported, I'm not even kidding."

"I'm not messing with her. I'm just getting something that doesn't belong to her."

"Whoa. Medal of courage to you," says Lexy. "That girl is *savage*."

I'm surprised how much sway Brooke holds over these three, who are clearly not wannabe popular girls, but I'm determined to get Jess's phone. I take a deep breath as we reach the top floor. "Just tell me which one is her room."

Annika points to a door on the left. "There it is. The Gates of Mordor." All three girls crack up.

"Is it locked?"

"Knowing Brooke and Mackenzie, it's probably booby-trapped," Nico says. So Brookenzie are roommates. That figures.

"Want us to stand guard?" asks Lexy.

"That would be awesome." I hesitate with my hand on the doorknob, conjuring visions of webcams and burglar alarms. Deported to *where*, I wonder. Antarctica? I picture myself in a thick parka, waddling over packed ice like a penguin. Okay. No use putting this off any longer. I take a deep breath and twist the knob.

Miraculously, the door opens. I look back at Annika and her two friends, mouthing "thank you," and slip inside.

Brookenzie's room looks like a boutique exploded. Designer clothes are all over the room, and I get the feeling the girls tried on eighteen outfits for last weekend's dance and couldn't be bothered with hangers. The floor is an obstacle course of designer shoes, with heels of all sizes and shapes. Both bedspreads are twisted and there's a wet towel with a *B* monogram dropped right on the floor, as if Brooke expected a hotel maid to come and pick up after her.

Both bedside tables are covered with makeup: Lancôme and Versace and Juicy Couture. There's a flat-screen TV the size of a blackboard, but what stops me short is the view from their window.

I thought the top floor of my middle school had a great view of the Manhattan skyline, but this is amazing. The school is so high on the cliffs that the river is way down below, like sparkling silk, and the George Washington Bridge is practically outside the window. No wonder Brooke wanted a room on the top floor. The Empire State Building must be her night-light.

I wouldn't have put up those curtains in ten million years. I'd sit up in bed every night and gaze out at the city.

But something else outside the window grabs my attention. A pair of tall blondes has come out of the dining hall — and they're heading this way! I've got to act fast!

Jason's noticed them, too. I can see him down there by the flower bed, trying to come up with some way to stall them.

There's no time to lose. I run my eyes over every surface. Which one is Brooke's desk? They're both such a mess that it's hard to tell. At last I spot Jess's red cell phone plugged into a charger, right next to a silver BlackBerry. Score! As I slip Jess's phone into my pocket, I pause. How did Brooke happen to have the right charger? Did she actually go out and *buy* one just so she could prank my best friend? This makes me so mad that I'm tempted to take Brooke's BlackBerry, too, just to teach her a lesson, but it seems like bad karma. Maybe I should write THOU SHALT NOT STEAL on the screen of her laptop in Perfect Pink nail polish.

Nice fantasy, but what I've got to do, *fast*, is get out of this room. Not a minute to spare. I open the door and hear voices outside in the stairwell.

"It's *them*," hisses Annika. I freeze. If I head down the stairs, I'll run smack into Brookenzie. If I stay where I am, I'll run into them *here*.

"Hide in our room," says Lexy. We scurry across the hall and duck into a bedroom that couldn't be more different. There are *three* beds, but even though the room feels more crowded, it's pretty and welcoming, with artwork and posters all over the walls and billowing scarves on the ceiling. I feel right at home.

"So? Did you get it?" asks Annika.

I nod. "Excellent!" she says, holding up her hand for a high five.

"You've got to get out of here ASAP," says Nico. "Brooke will go out of her mind if she sees that the cell is gone."

The thought sends a chill through my veins. There was such a jumble of papers and clothing on top of the desk that the charger was not in plain view, but what if she's planning to send a new photo this minute?

"Can we do a girl pack again?"

"Sure thing," says Annika, but it takes each girl a few moments to round up her things for afternoon classes. I'm climbing the walls with nervousness. Finally they're ready to go.

"Hey, guys," says Lexy. "Why don't I stay behind for a minute so there'll be the usual threesome? In case someone looks out the window."

"'Cause her hair looks nothing like yours," says Nico. "She might pass for Annika if they trade glasses."

"Yeah, right. And I'll fall down the stairs since I'm totally blind," says Annika. "Give her your hat."

Lexy takes a Bolivian rainbow-striped hat with earflaps off her desk lamp and tosses it to me. "There's only one person on campus who's cool enough to wear this hat. Now *that's* a disguise."

"Thanks," I say, twisting my hair up, pulling the cap on, and removing my glasses.

"Okay, *now*," says Annika. She and Nico go out first, and I fall in close behind them so no one we pass will be able to see my face. Luckily, nobody comes up the stairs as we're going back down.

Jason is waiting for us at the flower bed. "Lexy's llama hat — good one. Mission accomplished?"

I nod, patting my pocket. "One small step for womankind."

"Yes!" he says happily, punching the air.

We start walking away from the dorms, toward the clock tower. The weight of the phone in my pocket is comforting, but I've still got one hurdle: getting off campus. "How can I get past the gatehouse guard?" I ask.

"That's going to be tough any time before three," Jason says. "You need a signed note to get passes while class is in session."

"Is there a delivery entrance?"

"It's right next to Physical Plant. You see all these guys mowing lawns and stuff? That's where they keep their equipment. They'll be all over it."

"Especially now, with this crackdown on cutting," says Annika. "They've got teachers patrolling the grounds."

"One of them caught me before," I say. "I wound up in an earth science lecture."

"With Dr. Aran?" asks Nico.

"I don't know his name, but he *sounds like this*," I intone. "'That's hot molten *lava*, ladies and gentlemen.'"

Nico cracks up. "That's *perfect*. You nailed him!"

Nothing like getting a good review. But there's no time to bask.

"So where can I hide out until three?" I ask.

Jason, Nico, and Annika look at one another. "Last week, I'd say anywhere on the campus, but now?" Jason says. "They're really serious. No one, *no* one, is allowed out of class."

"The theatre? The gym?"

"There'll be classes in both of them. *Maybe* the library stacks, but Miss Lawler is like a Marine. I don't know how you'd get past her desk."

"How about the cafeteria?" I didn't get one single bite of my salad. I'm starved.

"I think your best bet's just to go to a classroom," says Annika. "There's only one period left after lunch; it's block scheduling."

"She's right," Nico says. "Come hang out with one of us."

"What do you have?"

"Trigonometry."

I shudder. I'm not even sure what trigonometry *is*, but

I know I'm allergic to math. I look over at Jason and Annika. "How about you?"

"We've got Latin," says Annika.

Help!

"I'll take my chance with the library stacks," I sigh.

"No, Latin is *perfect*," says Annika. "Mrs. Fass is two centuries old and she's blinder than me."

"We think Latin was her native language," says Jason. "She won't even know you're in the classroom."

"But I don't speak Latin!"

"Who does? It's a dead language," Annika says.

I'm still not convinced. "Does Brooke or Mackenzie take Latin?"

"No!" Jason and Annika say in unison.

"Okay, I'll try it. But if I get caught . . ."

"Trust me, you won't," says Annika. "This'll be fun."

I wish I agreed.

Chapter Nine

Jason and Annika take me into the classroom building through a side entrance, a few minutes late so the halls will be empty. I'm worried that this will draw more attention to us as we enter the classroom, but the teacher is just as they described her: white-haired and tiny, with heavy bifocals that slide down her nose. She's lettering words on a whiteboard, barely turning her head when we come into the room. Jason sits in the first row, and we head for the back.

"*Quisnam est tardus?*" Mrs. Fass says in a quavering voice.

Tardus, like tardy. I got that part, anyway.

"*Is est* Annika Reed," says Annika, signaling that I should sit next to her. A few students look surprised to see someone new in the classroom, but no one says anything. Most of them already look half asleep.

Mrs. Fass is doing a drill on verbs of motion, calling on students at random. It's just like being in Madame Lefkowitz's French class, except that I don't speak this language at *all*. I'm terrified.

What will I do if she calls on me? I rack my brains for anything I know in Latin. *Veni, vidi, vici*, or something like that. *E pluribus unum. Expelliarmus*. No, wait, that's from Harry Potter.

There must be some phrases from courtroom movies I've seen, like *habeas corpus* and . . . what else? Think *Law & Order*. Think *Legally Blonde*. What was that old Robin Williams movie Jess and I ordered on my Netflix? *Dead Poets Society*? He kept telling his students to *carpe diem*, seize the whatever.

"Alexa?" the teacher says, peering over her bifocals at me. She sounds very confused. "Lexy Davenport? Aren't you in my third period?"

"Um, Mrs. Fass?" starts a girl with braces, but Annika freezes her with a look and she backs off.

"Dentist appointment," I mumble, touching my teeth.

"Ah," she says. "Third person plural. To go."

Oh, God. Now what? Annika lifts a hand to her nose, muttering something behind it that I can't make out. All of a sudden I think of a phrase I remember from reading *Romeo and Juliet* in English class. It was part of the stage directions.

"*Exeunt omnes*," I say. Thank goodness for Shakespeare!

"And past tense?"

Oh, no. This is totally hopeless. *"Exeunted?"* Somebody snickers, and Mrs. Fass draws herself up like a miniature hawk.

"I suggest you spend less of your time drawing pictures in class and more of it studying," she says in a voice that's gone suddenly frosty. I wince as she moves on to somebody else. She's even harsher than Madame Lefkowitz.

The grammar drill goes on for what seems like forever, but luckily, she doesn't call on me — or rather, on Lexy — again. There are certain advantages to making stupid mistakes, I guess. People leave you alone.

Mrs. Fass just said something. Not to me, I hope, turning back toward her. No, it's to everyone, and it's a phrase to strike terror in my heart.

Pop quiz.

My blood starts to freeze in my veins as she hands a stack of blank paper to a bristle-haired boy in the front row. He passes one pile to the right and another behind him. In no time at all, it's come all the way back to our row.

I shoot Annika a look of sheer panic as I pass her the paper. "Copy off me," she mouths, and I nod. She angles her paper toward me on her desk, within easy view. Which is fine, but whose name do I put in the corner? I start sweating under my blazer. I'm not about to write down *Diana Donato*, and I wouldn't want Lexy to get stuck with *my* grade on this quiz. Anyway, she probably took it third period.

I hesitate, my pen in the air, and then realize something amazing. I don't have to turn this quiz in! I'm not getting graded. I'm not in this class, or even at this *school*. If I just keep moving my pen and look busy throughout, no one will suspect me, and when we pass our papers forward, I'll just leave mine out of the pile. Sneak it onto my lap, tuck it under my blazer, and toss it. No problem.

Holding back a smile at my sudden change of luck, I write *Juliet Capulet* in the upper right corner and sit with my pen poised, waiting for the first question.

"He went." *Ex post facto*, I write.

"They watched him go." *Xbox factor*.

"We arrived at the coliseum." *Stadium Arcadium*, I write, barely able to keep from giggling. Annika glances at me, probably wondering why I'm enjoying myself.

"He carried his sword." *Carrie Underwood*.

And so it goes, twenty-five questions and twenty-five answers of pure, utter nonsense. If only I got to do this on my French tests!

The rest of the students look tense and unhappy, and I get the feeling that nobody actually knows all the answers. From the way the kids grumble and shift in their seats, it even seems possible that this strange little nearsighted woman is quizzing them on things she's never gone over in class, which has happened to me more than once. If you're taking a test where your grade really matters, that totally stinks. And if you're enrolled in the kind of competitive, grade-grubbing prep school where people start pressuring you about law school when you're only thirteen, it must be even worse. Who takes Latin and trigonometry in eighth grade anyway?

I look around at the rows of stressed-looking students, all dressed alike, and feel a sudden wave of affection for Weehawken Middle School. Prep school is not seeming so cool after all. I'm very relieved when we pass papers forward (not counting mine, of course; that one slides onto my lap) and the final bell rings. I can't wait to get back through that gatehouse.

"What were you *writing*?" Annika asks as we head back out into the hall. "Show me that quiz."

I hand her my paper, and as she reads down the list of answers, she starts laughing harder and harder. "Ig-pay Atin-lay? Carpe Jack Sparrow? You just went off the deep end!"

I'm glad she thinks I'm funny, but we're back out in public now, and I'm worried that her snorts of laughter may draw attention to us. All I need is to run into Brooke and Mackenzie again, this time with Jess's cell phone in my pocket. I look around nervously, trying to signal to Annika to keep her voice down. But the voice that stops me in my tracks is a boy's.

"Hey, Lexy Davenport. *Not*. Who are *you*?" It's the bristle-haired boy from the front row who handed out quiz papers. He has arching dark eyebrows, and all of a sudden I recognize him as one of the boys who walked into the dance with Brookenzie. My breathing gets shallow. I've been discovered.

"Get over yourself, Duncan," Annika snaps. "She's a friend of mine."

"I asked you a question," he says to me. "What were you doing in Latin class, Exeunted?"

"I'm . . . I'm thinking of transferring here," I blurt.

"But she won't if the boys act like jerks. So back off." Annika clamps her hand on to my arm and leads me down the hall toward the back staircase.

I whisper to Annika, my voice frantic. "That boy is friends with —"

"I know," she says. "Oops. There they are." Sure enough, towering above the cluster of students in front of us, I see two matching blond heads.

And they're coming right toward me!

Without missing a beat, Annika drops her pencil. "Bend over and get it," she hisses.

"But what if —"

"They'll just see the llama hat." Raising her voice, she says, "Lexy, you dropped your pencil."

Against every instinct, I crouch down on hands and knees, scrabbling to pick up the pencil that's rolled toward the wall. Suddenly I realize my paint-stained right sleeve is completely exposed. What if they notice? I twist that arm under my body and reach for the pencil with my left, feeling even more awkward.

I see two pairs of designer shoes clicking over the parquet floor, getting closer and closer. My heart rises into my throat as they stop right in front of me. I hear Mackenzie's scornful, "Look who's crawling!"

"Don't pick on Lexy," says Annika.

"Loser," Brooke's voice sneers, and the shoes click on past me.

Loser. Just like her text message. I'm so angry I feel like tackling her from behind, but that wouldn't be wise. The main thing that matters is getting away, and I figure we've got about seven seconds until they reach Duncan and he tells them both I'm not Lexy. I can't take any more. I jump up and bound toward the back stairs with Annika, frantically dodging around other kids in the hall.

"Watch it!" says someone as we career past.

We charge down the stairs about three at a time and propel ourselves out of the building. Jason is waiting for us, and we all run pell-mell toward the gatehouse, dodging behind the newly clipped hedge so we're hidden from view. We sprint to the end of the driveway.

"What are we going to do now?" I pant.

"You two keep walking, and I'll sign all three of us out," Jason says.

"But there'll only be two of you coming back in."

"No worries," says Annika. "I'll come back later with Lexy and she'll tell the night guard she forgot to sign in. Piece of cake."

"Ready?" says Jason and both of us nod. He walks up to the gatehouse window and asks for the sign-out sheet. Annika positions herself between me and the guard, "just in case," and we walk through the gate side by side.

It feels great to be outside that fence. We see cars of all sorts driving past, people dressed in whatever they want to be wearing. Not a single plaid skirt or blue blazer in sight.

I pull off Lexy's llama hat and return it to Annika, shaking my hair loose. A few moments later, Jason joins us alongside the fence. "So it's all good?"

"Never better. Thank you so much," I say. "Both of you."

"No problem," says Annika. "Say hi to Elise, okay? Maybe I'll see you again when I pick that thing up from the cleaners." She gestures toward my — I mean *her* — paint-stained uniform.

"That would be great," I tell her.

"Take care," Jason says. "And hey? Please give Jess that phone right away, because I'm going to call her the second she gets it."

I hurry as fast as I can, but it's still way past three by the time I get back to the ice cream stand. Will Cat still be waiting?

141

I skid into the parking lot with my heart pounding. The space where she promised she'd meet me is empty. I look left and right, but there's no van in sight.

What am I going to do now? I stand in the parking lot, panting hard, my chest rising and falling with every breath. My hand closes over Jess's phone in my pocket, and I suddenly feel as if I'm going to burst into tears.

Before I do, though, I hear the sound of an engine starting behind me. I turn just as Cat drives the van from around the back of the ice cream stand, where she's been waiting. She drives alongside me and rolls down the window.

"You took long enough. I was freaking out."

"Cat, I'm so sorry."

"Just get in," she says. "You can tell me the rest while we're driving."

I circle around to the passenger side and climb in. Cat's gathered my school clothes and piled them up on the floor by my feet. "Seat belt," she says. "Come on, we're already way late."

I fasten my seat belt and try one more time to apologize.

"I *thought* about leaving you here when it got to be ten after three," Cat says as she turns the steering wheel. "But I was too worried about you." She looks at me. "So? Did you get what you came for?"

"I did." I take Jess's red phone from my pocket and show it to her.

"Well, that's good, at least," says Cat. "But you're the one telling your dad why we're so late to work."

"Absolutely," I tell her. But I've got a phone call to make first.

Jess shrieks when I tell her. "I can't believe this!" she keeps saying over and over. It's so great to hear her voice sounding happy again. I couldn't stand her being mad at me.

"I'm not sure I believe it myself, and I was there." I tell her the whole story, complete with impersonations of all the weird teachers at Foreman.

Finally, Cat interrupts.

"Listen, I don't mean to break this up, but, Diana, you gotta get out of that uniform. Want me to pull into a parking lot?"

"I think I can manage." I tell Jess good-bye, then

wriggle around in my seat belt, shrugging out of the blazer and blouse and pulling my sweater back over my cami, unpinning the plaid skirt and sliding on my favorite leggings.

It feels really good to be me again. Not Annika Reed, or Lexy Davenport, or anyone else who might go to the Foreman Academy. Just a tired, happy girl with some really good friends, and an after-school job at her family's dry cleaners.

Chapter Ten

Dad is out making sales calls around Newark Airport, trying to round up some airline and restaurant uniform business. This should make me happy — he's clearly determined to solve this money crunch without cutting anyone's job — but the short-term result is that Miss MacInerny's in charge when Cat and I punch the time clock a full half hour late.

Cat tries to concoct an excuse about Jared's van breaking down on the way, but I've stretched the truth enough times for one day. When MacInerny looks over at me, all I can manage is, "I'm really sorry." Joyless sends Cat to the back room to sort and bag orders, and I take a cart full of clothes from Elise, who's working the customer counter. As I push it through the doors into the workroom,

I hear Elise say, "Oh, wait," and tell MacInerny she'll be right back.

"What?" I say when Elise catches up with me behind the closed doors. I expect her to call my attention to something that needs Special Care, or a garment that hasn't been tagged yet. Instead she whispers, "Did you meet my cousin?"

"I did. She was awesome!"

Elise nods and smiles. "Let me know if you need any help." She slips back out to the customer counter so quickly, it takes me a second to realize honest Elise has just offered to help with a cover-up story.

I might need her help, too. I still have to sneak Annika's uniform back into Special Care so Rose can remove its red paint stains, put the white blouse through for a second cleaning, and hang it back up on the Dress Parade. Thank goodness the customer hasn't come in yet to claim it! When Nelson "borrows" outfits overnight, he always makes sure to return them first thing in the morning. "Cover your tracks *fast*," he tells me. "And never lie more than you have to."

I have to get Nelson to re-stitch the sleeves before I bring the blazer to Rose. Loretta and Sadie stay out of his business, so that's not a problem, but I'm terrified that MacInerny will catch him and start asking questions.

"Are you sure you can do this now?" I ask as he turns up a sleeve.

"What, you mean work on a customer's garment?" Nelson threads his needle in one quick move. "That *is* what I'm paid for."

I gulp. "I don't want to get you in trouble." Should I tell him what I overheard?

Nelson arches an eyebrow. "Did I ever tell you the nickname I had when I worked as a line cook? The waitresses called me 'Exempt.'"

"Why was that?"

Nelson's fingers fly over the hem. I can't believe he can make such perfect stitches so quickly. "I broke every rule in the kitchen. I even went out and sat down with friends in the customer section when I had my whites on. The other cooks couldn't believe my nerve." He shrugs. "What were they gonna do, fire me?"

I wince. "Have you ever been fired?"

Nelson snips off a stray thread of lining silk. "I don't stay long at a job I don't like. I'm like a cat burglar, gone before they catch hold of me. I wasn't cut out to work in a kitchen. I'm a hundred percent *Project Runway* and zero *Top Chef*. If I'm in a restaurant, I wanna be holding the menu."

"What are you doing, Mr. Martinez?" It's Joyless's voice right behind me, demanding an answer. I'm petrified. My mouth tries to open, but no words come out.

Nelson is as calm as a Zen master. "This excellent worker noticed a ripped hem the customer must have forgotten to mention." He holds up the blazer's left sleeve and shows Miss MacInerny what he's just done. "Good eye, Diana."

MacInerny narrows her eyes at me, but all she says is, "Well, don't stand there waiting too long. We're getting backed up."

"Almost finished," Nelson assures her. When she withdraws, he takes a last few swift stitches, snips off the thread and hands me the blazer. "There you go. Ready for Rose. And you owe me a favor."

"Any time," I say, hoping he'll keep this job for a long time to come. "Just say the word, and I'm there for you."

Nelson smiles. "I'm counting on it."

It's good to be back.

Dad's in a wonderful mood at dinner. He spoke to dozens of prospective clients, and he picked up one right on the spot, a rental car franchise whose employees wear matching maroon blazers. "I'm telling you, there's a gold mine out there," he says. "How many businesses in north Jersey dress their employees in uniforms? I'm going to hit every mall, every theme park, every hotel. . . . Tomorrow I'm going to drive out to Meadowlands Stadium and find out who dry-cleans the Giants."

His joy is contagious, or maybe the box of Swiss chocolates he bought at the airport put everyone in a good mood. Whatever the reason, the twins aren't whiny, and when I ask Fay if I can walk over to Jess's as soon as I'm done cleaning up, she says yes right away.

"Thanks so much," I say, giving her an impulsive quick hug. She looks very surprised, and more than a little bit pleased. I can feel Dad beaming at me.

Later, halfway up the hill, with Jess's phone in my pocket, I realize I have a decision to make. That cell phone is chock-full of photos I took at the dance, including that horrible one with Jess making a fish face and Jason right next to her, holding his nose. Thank God I got the phone back before Brooke hit SEND on *that* one! Should I go through and delete all the dance photos? Jess would have no way of knowing they'd ever been there, and I wouldn't have to confess that I'd taken her phone out, and might not have zipped it back in. After all, did Jess show me those photos of me in my green smock before she deleted them? No way. She just hit the DELETE button sight unseen, and I'm eternally grateful.

I take out the phone and power it up, then review the full album of photos. There are the pictures we took of ourselves getting dressed, then the two in the Foreman Academy bathroom, and the rest. I'm about to delete them when I take a closer look. Some of these photos are *good*. Jess might really like to have pictures of Jason, or the two of them dancing together. And even the ones that aren't good, like that embarrasing holding-his-nose shot, are part of the story of our night at Foreman.

Plus I don't want to look my best friend in the eye and know that I haven't told her the whole truth.

I turn the phone off and climb the rest of the way up the hill. Dash opens the door when I knock, says "Yuck," and pretends to shut it in my face.

"Very funny," I say, wedging it open with one of my Converse. He turns and yells, "Jess! It's for you," with the accent on *it*.

"Thank you, Dashiell," I say, and he makes a face. He can't stand his full name.

Jess comes barreling downstairs, her eyes bright. "Do you have it?"

I hold up the phone and she grabs it, switching it on right away. "Yay! Diana, thank you! I can't wait to hear the messages Jason left!"

"There's something else on there, too," I say.

We go up to her room, flop across her bed, and I tell her everything. I start with the photos I sneaked while she and Jason were dancing. Then I take a deep breath and admit that I *might* not have zipped the phone back in its pocket, and that I was afraid she would hate me if I told the truth. I hang my head and hold my breath, wondering if she'll understand.

"Okay," says Jess after a moment, putting her hand on

151

my shoulder. "First of all, there's nothing on earth that could make me hate you. We're besties forever. Got that?"

I nod, feeling a warmth that spreads all the way up from my toes.

Jess goes on. "Second of all, what you did today was beyond amazing. I can't believe you snuck into Foreman! And went into Brookenzie's *room*. And took a Latin test! Even though you turn into Jell-O whenever you hear the words 'Take out your pencil.'" Jess looks a little choked up and we squeeze hands. "I mean, you did all that . . . for me. What can I say except . . . thanks?"

"You are so welcome," I tell her, and mean every word. I feel a little choked up myself.

She holds up the phone. "So can I play my messages now?"

I grin ear to ear. "You better!"

I wake up the next morning and can't wait to go to school. First-period gym with Amelia is actually *fun*, even without any fencing equipment or outdoor lacrosse fields. And after the true torture chamber of Mrs. Fass, Madame Lefkowitz doesn't drive me as crazy as usual. At the end of the class, she passes back our corrected French tests. In the old days, I would have tensed up like a rubber band, but now that I've goofed my way through that Latin quiz, I feel much more chill. There are worse things on earth than not knowing the French word for *wastebasket*.

When she hands me my test, I'm astonished to find out I got an A-minus. All that worrying over nothing! If this was a musical, I'd spread my arms wide and burst into song. *C'est fantastique!*

At lunch, even the the limp cafeteria fries taste better today. I'm just happy to be in a place I belong, surrounded by friends at our usual chipped-linoleum table, talking and laughing and stealing one another's desserts. It was cool to get an inside look at the Land of the Preps, and I hope I'll stay friends with Jason and Annika, but the truth is, I wouldn't trade places. Not even if somebody paid me.

When Jess pulls out her cell phone to show Sara and Amelia a picture of Jason, it's one of the nice ones we left when we went through the photos together last night and deleted the "Rock Lobster" fish face (which Jess agreed was her personal nightmare come true).

"Wow!" Sara gushes. "He really *does* look like Nick Jonas." Jess blushes bright pink.

"He's a really great guy," I confirm, and that nagging little feeling of envy I felt at the dance is nowhere to be found. I feel nothing but joy for my friend.

Jess clicks through several more pictures of Jason while Sara and Amelia *ooh*, *aah*, and tease her. Then Jess calls over to Will, who's sitting nearby with a table of boys. "Hey, rock star! Come see this picture of you!"

Now it's my turn to blush. I wish we'd deleted that, too, but it's such a good shot. The stage lights hit the back of his head in a really dramatic way, and he's got that intent, focused look you see in real concert photos.

Will ambles over to look. "You took this?" he asks Jess, and she points at me.

"*Rolling Stone* cover photo by Diana Donato," she tells him.

"Cool," he says, and goes back to his table. He's doing his man-of-few-words thing again, but I could swear he looks secretly pleased. Anyway, now that I've seen the real Will with a bass guitar in his hands, his shyness just makes me smile.

154

Jess hands over her cell phone and shows me the very last photo, which we took last night in her bedroom. Jess and I are side by side with our arms around each other's shoulders, grinning like the best friends we are. And that makes me feel better than anything else.

Even acing a French test.

Turn the page for a sneak peek at

#3: Rock & Role

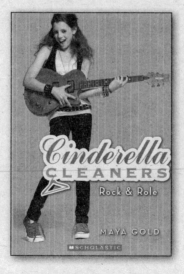

I cut through the parking lot between Sam's and the cleaners. It still gives me a thrill to go in the employee entrance, like a real insider. I stash my backpack in my locker, pin my name tag onto my smock, and go into the workroom. The machine noise and chemical smells don't startle me like they used to. I've got it *down*.

Elise flashes me a smile as MacInerny greets me with her usual sucking-on-lemons "Good afternoon." Somehow, with just two words, she can manage to make me feel like I'm late when I'm not, or that I've already screwed up something I haven't started yet. I had a math teacher like that last year. You were guilty until proven innocent.

There's a cart full of clothes that need to go back to the workroom, so I assume that'll be my first job. But before I can roll it out, MacInerny hands me a man's jacket and says, "Bring this to tailoring."

I smile. Any workday that starts with a visit to Nelson is fine with me. Then I notice the cuffs are rolled up inside out, with safety pins jabbed through the fabric — the customer must have marked it himself. "Nelson's not going to like this. He'll want a live measure."

"Nelson's not here," MacInerny says curtly. The breath goes out of my lungs as if someone just punched me. It couldn't have happened that fast. Could it? Maybe she just means Nelson's not here *today*.

"Where is he?" I ask, but MacInerny has already turned toward the next customer waiting in line, flashing her fake-friendly smile. I look at Elise, who shakes her head, clueless. She comes to work straight from high school, arriving just minutes before me, so how would she know?

Clutching the jacket, I carry it into the tailoring section. Nelson is nowhere in sight, but both white-haired seamstresses look up from their sewing machines. "Hello, gorgeous," Sadie intones, turning her head toward Loretta. "Is she a vision or what?"

"She's a vision," Loretta rasps, nodding.

"Where's Nelson?" I ask.

They look at each other. "Haven't you heard?" Sadie says.

"Heard what? Where is he?" I'm starting to panic.

"The word is he's taking some personal time." Sadie raises both hands from her sewing machine, crooking her first two fingers into quote marks.

"What does that mean? Is he coming back?" I'm so upset I can barely control my voice. How could Dad *do* this? Nelson is not just the head of the tailoring section, he's its heart and soul. Loretta and Sadie have great sewing skills — they've both worked here for decades — but Nelson's the one with the designer's eye. He's the go-to guy for fixing things, even when they seem impossible. And he's my friend. I can't stand the thought of working at Cinderella Cleaners without him.

"You know what we know," Sadie shrugs. "Personal time, and I quote."

"Such a talented boy," says Loretta. She holds out her hand for the jacket, frowning. "What kind of klutz pinned these cuffs?"

I ask everyone in the workroom if they've heard anything more about Nelson. The rumors are flying. He quit, he got fired, someone made him an offer he couldn't refuse. Cat comes in a few minutes late, and she's as upset as I am. Nelson's her best bud. He designed both our dresses when we got to sneak into a Broadway opening, and he and Cat love to gossip and crack jokes in Spanish. "I can't believe he'd take off without saying *hasta luego*," she says. "That's not like him at all." She looks like she's going to burst into tears.

That does it. I put down the orders I'm sorting and march to my father's office. I need to get to the bottom of this.

Dad's sitting at his big desk, on what seems like a customer service call. He winks at me, gesturing that I should sit, but I don't. "Yes, of course," he says into the phone. "I understand. . . . Right. I'll send somebody out right away." He rolls his eyes at me, letting me know that he's talking with someone impossible. "Of course. Not a problem . . . Well, that's what we're here for." He hangs up and sighs. Then his face brightens. "How are *you*, honey?"

"Where's Nelson?" I ask without prelude.

"He's taking some personal time," says Dad automatically.

"What does that *mean*? Did you fire him?"

Dad looks affronted. "Of course not. He told me he needed some time to pursue other projects, and I let him have it, even though he gave no notice at all."

That's a surprise. This was Nelson's idea?

I look at Dad. He wouldn't lie to me. Not about something like this. "So that means he'll be coming back, right?"

Dad sighs. "I suppose that depends on the other projects." He isn't meeting my eye, and I can't help remembering the conversation I overheard, when his accountant advised him to let someone go, and suggested "that tailor Martinez."

"Did he say what he's doing?"

"Diana, I've said all I can. It's enough." So he knows, but he's not going to tell me. I can read Dad like a book, and he knows it. He's looking at me as if he's considering something. Maybe if I look angelic enough, he'll let me know more.

Dad leans back in his chair. "Can I entrust you with something?"

Oh, good. Here it is. I nod eagerly. "Sure!"

"I just got off the phone with a client. You know Mrs. Felter?" Of course I do. Everyone knows Mrs. Felter — she's here twice a week, always making some special demand or complaining about something somebody did wrong. But what has that got to do with Nelson? Is he doing some special project for *her*?

Dad goes on. "She dropped something off for her daughter this morning, same-day service, and can't pick it up by the end of the workday. I need someone to walk it down to her building. It's only a few blocks away — you know RiverVista Estates?"

Of course I do! Has he forgotten how much Mom hated those condo deve lopments, with their tall towers blocking the view for the rest of us? When I was little, she dragged me to committee meetings and sat at the ShopRite with petitions to stop RiverVista. I hated it then, but if I could have even an hour of that time with my mother again, I'd never complain about anything.

Dad mistakes my hesitation. "You don't have to go to her apartment, just drop it off with the doorman downstairs. Or I can ask Cat or Elise."

"No, it's fine," I say quickly. The truth is, I'd love a walk. And even if I hate the towers, their view of the Manhattan skyline is stunning.

Dad smiles. "That's my girl." He opens the door of his office and leads me out to the customer counter. "Diana is making a special delivery," he announces to Joyless. "She'll be back in a half hour or so."

I slip out of my smock as Dad steps on the pedal that sends the conveyor belt of bagged garments swishing around the ceiling, what I called the Dress Parade when I was little. I wonder what pantsuit or stiff evening dress Mrs. Felter needs ASAP. Dad stops the belt and takes down a clear plastic bag. My jaw drops.

Inside is the cutest vest I've ever seen. It's dark blue with a deep scoop neck, tiny lapels, and a pieced satin back, with a row of adorable miniature buttons. It's totally not Mrs. Felter's taste — I'd wear it myself, to a rock concert. Where did she *find* it? And why did she buy something so young and hip? Then I remember Dad telling me she dropped it off for her daughter.

Lucky daughter.

Dad prints the receipt and shows me the address. "Nikki Felter," he says, handing over the vest. "Have fun." He gives me a hug, and I take special pleasure in going outside through the customers-only door, right under Joyless's nose.

The breeze catches the plastic bag like a sail, and I drape

it over my shoulder, hooking my thumb through the top of the hanger. I haven't gone ten steps from the cleaners when I run smack into the last person I would expect to see: Will Carson!

He's coming from Sam's Diner, holding a cardboard tray full of cups. We stare at each other in shock. Then I blurt out a line that's so obvious I'd groan out loud if I had to say it in a play: "What are you *doing* here?"

Will's answer isn't much better. "Um, getting drinks?" He holds the tray up for proof. Funny, I guessed that part.

"Thirsty much?" Will looks confused or uncomfortable, I can't tell which. Did he not get the joke? I point. Two milkshakes, a Coke, and a coffee. Oh, never mind. "Who's all that for?"

"Oh. Just some people. My dad." He looks nervously over my shoulder. "So this is . . . I thought you worked closer to school."

"No, I take the bus." Boy, *that* was interesting. Shy must be catching.

Will nods, shuffling his feet as the wind blows his hair over his forehead. He reaches up, brushing it off, and it blows right back down. "So, see you later." He starts to walk past me and looks disconcerted when I head the same way.

I lift up the hanger, explaining, "Delivery. Where is your dad?"

"He's . . . um, over there." He makes a vague gesture toward the river.

"Me, too!" I blush. "I mean, that's where I'm *going*."

Will nods, but says nothing. We wait for the green light, then cross and walk most of a block without saying a word. I'm racking my brain for some way to make conversation. "Isn't your dad a musician?"

"Yeah." Silence. We keep on walking.

"What instrument?"

"He was a drummer."

Was? "What is he doing now?"

Will stops walking suddenly, turning to face me. "Can you keep a secret?" I'm so surprised by his intensity that I just nod. "It's a really big secret. Like, *huge*."

"I swear," I say. "I won't tell anyone."

Will takes a deep breath. "He's a sound engineer."

That doesn't seem like much of a secret. I look at him, waiting for more. Will sighs. "On Tasha Kane's video."

My eyeballs bulge out of my head. I shriek, "WHAT?"

"You promised," Will says quickly. "You can't tell *anyone*."

"Your father is working with *Tasha Kane*?" He just said so, but I can't believe my ears. Huge doesn't cover it. This is beyond huge; it's epic. I look at the tray full of drinks in Will's hands and blurt, "Are those for *her*?"

He grins. "No way. She's got a P.A. to take care of her." I'm proud to recognize the inside slang for Production Assistant. "These are for the sound booth."

Somehow we've started walking again. My heart's pounding high up in my throat and my mind's full of so many questions I don't know where to begin. I can't believe someone I know — and let's face it, who I sort of like — is hanging around in the sound booth for Tasha Kane's video!

I'm totally freaking myself, but I don't want to show it when Will seems so cool with all this. He's actually gotten less mumbly and shy — like he was with a bass in his hands. Maybe just being around music makes him more relaxed.

"So where are they shooting?" Will darts me a look. "I won't tell. I already promised." It's got to be close by, since Will is on foot.

"The soundstage is inside a warehouse. They're keeping it all under wraps because Tasha gets *mobbed* by fans. You can't imagine."

Actually, I can. I was backstage at a Broadway opening and saw all the fans leaning over the rail to get autographs from Adam Kessler, the star. Tasha's about six billion times more famous, though. "How did your dad get to work for her?"

"He's friends with her manager. That's why we moved here from Santa Fe." Will has stopped walking. He's standing outside the old Standard Carpet warehouse, which looks . . . like an old carpet warehouse. If they're trying to keep a low profile, they're doing a wonderful job. I notice a few improbably glossy cars parked on the street, and some new-looking bolts on the side entrance. Could it be?

I point over Will's shoulder, raising my eyebrows. He nods. "But you really —"

"I know," I say quickly. "Your secret is safe."

He looks at the cleaner bag I'm holding over my shoulder. "How far do you have to take that?"

I swivel and point at the glass-and-chrome tower that looms from the skyline a few blocks away. "The Hideous Vista."

"So would you have time to . . . I mean, if you wanted . . ." Why is he mumbling *now*? I'm holding my breath. Will looks down at his feet, takes a deep breath, and raises his eyes to look right into mine. "Do you want to come in with me?"

Oh. My. God.

"YES!"

"Come on," says Will, and we start toward the door. A sudden breeze catches the cleaner bag and I realize I'm going to feel like an idiot taking it into the soundstage. But what can I do? I can't very well hang it out here on the chain-link fence. Someone might steal Nikki Felter's supercool rock 'n' roll vest. Unless. . . .

"What is it?" Will asks, and I realize my steps have slowed.

"I don't want to bring this inside."

"Oh," says Will. "I don't think anyone cares."

I care. If I'm going to meet Tasha Kane, I don't want to be clutching a dry cleaner bag. And I'd like to show *some* sense of style, not the boring striped tank top and skinny jeans I pulled from my dresser this morning. If I put on Nikki's vest, no one could steal it. Right?

"Just a minute," I say to Will, and before he can ask what I'm doing, I've hung up the bag on the fence, reached inside it, and shimmied the vest off its hanger. I slip it on over my tank top. It fits as if it was made for me.

"Cool," says Will, and he leads me to the door. As we get closer, I notice a state-of-the-art security camera and intercom system you wouldn't find on most buildings designed to store shag rugs. I hold Will's tray of drinks while he punches in a code and gives both our names to the intercom. The door buzzes open. Right inside are a pair of massive security guards.

"You, I got," says the first. "You're Tyler Carson's kid. Who's your company?"

"A friend from school," says Will.

"Sign in," says the guard, and I do. The second guard passes a metal detector wand over us. He's not at all scary — I don't think Will and I look like much of a threat — but I'm extra glad I didn't bring in a dry cleaning bag on a wire hanger.

"Okay, you're cool," says the guard. "Keep it quiet, they're taping."

They're *taping*? Wow! This is amazing!

I follow Will down a hall with a lot of doors. Where do they go? Who's behind them? This feels so *backstage*. Finally we get to a door with a red light above it. Will and I pause. I can hear one of Tasha's recordings being played — at least that's what I think I'm hearing, till someone says, "Cut!" and the music stops. The red light goes off.

I look at Will, wide-eyed. That was *live*! "Quick," he says. "They're between takes." He swings open the door to the sound booth, and we slip inside.

The booth is much bigger than I would have guessed, filled with racks of recording and mixing equipment. The whole front is glass, and the scene I can see through the window looks like something out of a DVD special feature. The band is theatrically lit, and the lead guitarist is mopping the sweat from his forehead. The drummer is chugging a bottle of water. There are crew guys in baseball caps, and camera technicians rolling their rigs back into place for the next take. And right in the center is Tasha Kane, standing patiently still as a makeup girl brushes her face.

She can't be more than ten yards away. I stare at her, mesmerized by every detail. She's wearing a peacock blue top over leggings and ankle boots, with a studded black belt and a really cool necklace that looks like a giant charm bracelet. Her hair is pulled back from her forehead with a triple-strand headband, and it tumbles around her pretty face in a pile of black curls. She's shorter in person than I would have guessed, and her skin is the color of butterscotch toffee. Even standing still, she's magnetic. I can't take my eyes off her.

Will slides the coffee in front of a man who must be his father. He's wearing a headset, his face lit by rows of controls. He nods a quick thanks while listening to somebody over the headset. "Got it," he says, rubbing the bridge of his nose. "Yeah, I'm on it." He moves a few levers.

Will passes a milkshake to a technician with shoulder-length dreads and the Coke to a woman in black with a dragon tattooed on one shoulder. He comes back to join me, taking a sip from the second milkshake. "Want some? It's vanilla." He holds out the cup.

Only a boy could think about food at a moment like this. I shake my head, studying Tasha. Will smiles. I can tell he's enjoying my view of his world. It's hard to imagine that this could be somebody's version of visiting Dad at the office. It makes watching the Dress Parade seem pretty puny.

The drummer runs a stick over the snare drum, pumping one foot up and down in a trickle of rhythm. All three cameras are back in their places. An English–accented voice that must be the director's comes over an intercom. "Okay, let's do another. You ready?" Tasha nods, and the makeup girl scurries off to the sidelines. A young woman holding a clapper slate takes her place. I hear a familiar set of commands that I've only heard in a movie: "Roll tape . . ." "Rolling . . ." "Action!"

And suddenly I'm at a Tasha Kane concert! The drummer slaps into a groove, the keyboard player lets loose a dance riff, and Tasha is strutting and singing, her unmistakable voice sounding just like it does on the radio. The song has a chorus so catchy that I want to sing along with it the first time I'm hearing the words.

"Have you heard?" Tasha sings. "Have you heard, heard the word?"

One of the cameras is swooping around her as she sings and dances, and a man with a mike boom follows her every move. How can she concentrate with all that equipment so close to her? She's really a pro. And her dance moves are awesome.

"Cut!" says the voice on the intercom. Everything shuts down at once. Tasha looks disappointed. The drummer groans. Inside the booth, the guy with the dreadlocks slumps back in his chair. "What are we on, take sixteen?"

"My bad, people," comes through the intercom. "How about a ten-minute break?"

"Make it fifteen," Tasha says.

"For you, darling, twenty."

"All *right*," says Will's father, stretching his arms. He turns in his swivel chair, smiling at me. "Welcome to the exciting world of recording."

"This is Diana," says Will. "She works at the cleaners next to the diner."

For the first time since we came inside, I remember I'm

supposed to be working. "I better go," I tell Will. "My dad'll get worried if I'm gone too long."

"It's a dad thing," says Will's father, winking. "Nice meeting you."

"Thank you *so* much," I say. "This was amazing."

Will puts down his milkshake and opens the door of the sound booth. As we step into the hall, I'm shocked to see a familiar peacock blue top coming right toward me. It's Tasha!

She smiles at Will like she's seen him before, but isn't quite sure of his name. She glances at me, then looks back with an intent expression.

"Cool vest!" she says. "Where did you get that?"

Blushing bright red, I stammer, "Um . . . it was a gift."

Well, sort of.

She narrows her eyes, studying the cut of Nikki Felter's vest, then turns to the woman beside her, who must be her assistant. "See, this is the look I want Ingrid to do. Can I bring you to wardrobe?"

Who, me? I must look totally dumbstruck, because Tasha says, "Sorry, I don't know your name."

"It's Diana," I manage to stutter.

"Diana." She smiles. "Follow me for a minute?"

"Sure!" I say. Yes, I am already late, and yes, Dad's going to worry, but she's *Tasha Kane*! I can't believe that I'm *talking* to her, much less following her down the hall to the wardrobe department.

You belong at

WILDWOOD STABLES

Friendship, rivalry, and the amazing place that
brings them together . . . Read them all!

#1: Daring to Dream

#2: Playing for Keeps

#3: Racing Against Time

#4: Learning to Fly

candy Apple Books

Drama Queen

I've Got a Secret

Confessions of a
Bitter Secret Santa

The Boy Next Door   The Sweetheart Deal   The Sister Switch   Snowfall Surprise

The Accidental
Cheerleader

The Babysitting Wars

Star-Crossed

Read them all!

Accidentally
Fabulous

Accidentally
Famous

Accidentally
Fooled

Accidentally
Friends

How to Be a Girly Girl
in Just Ten Days

Miss Popularity

Miss Popularity
Goes Camping

Making Waves

Life, Starring Me!

Juicy Gossip

Callie for President

Totally Crushed